WIRED FEAR

PARADISE CRIME THRILLERS BOOK 8

TOBY NEAL

Darkness cannot drive out darkness; only light can do that. Hate cannot drive out hate; only love can do that.
- Dr. Martin Luther King, Jr.

CHAPTER ONE

Day One

REVENGE WAS BEST SEASONED with anticipation.

Akane Chang opened the locked metal box his cousin handed him. His favorite weapons lay nestled in dense foam: a combat blade in a scabbard, a sleek Ruger 1911 semi-auto pistol with a box of ammo.

He took the knife out of the box and drew it from its sheath. He waved it back and forth. Blue fire gleamed along its honed edge.

So many good times with that blade...

Akane glanced at his cousin, District Attorney Alan Chang, a man with a lot to lose if his role in helping Akane escape ever came to light. Alan Chang had provided access and intel to members of their crime syndicate, who'd sprung Akane during transport to the county jail after his trial.

"I'm only doing this because I think the family needs you." Alan wet his lips. "This can't ever come back on me."

"Of course, it won't come back on you." Akane smiled. "I owe you. And it's good to have me owe you."

"What's your plan?" Pearls of sweat dotted the DA's forehead and his eyes hadn't left the blade as Akane played with it.

"Better that you don't know." Akane tested the blade's sharpness on a callous on his thumb. The skin sliced off as easy as butter.

"Well then. Your new ID and some cash are right over there." Alan pointed a latex-gloved hand toward a wallet resting on the apartment's side table. "Don't call me. Don't contact me."

"Surprised you didn't wear a hair net and crime scene booties when you came to visit," Akane mocked.

Alan stared at him resentfully. "I was never here, you understand?"

Akane didn't respond. Alan Chang was in a handy position as DA. That position would be even better if he got a judgeship—and while he still wanted something, Akane had leverage on him. Didn't mean they had to like each other.

"Good luck." The DA left as silently as he'd come, locking the door.

Akane loaded the Ruger, enjoying the click of the heavy cartridges as he filled the magazine, the smell of gun oil, the solid heft of the pistol in his hand. He'd felt so powerless throughout the trial. *No more.*

He had a revenge list half a dozen names long. His brother Byron's name would have been right at the top if someone hadn't already offed him. Now that Byron was out of the way, that bitch female investigator and her asshole partner who'd testified against him had moved up.

But first he needed to keep his eye on the ball and make sure his position as head of the family was locked down. To that end, he had messages out to the leaders of the Changs' gambling, drug dealing, and prostitution networks. Once he was in charge on the Big Island, Akane could take all the time he wanted to hunt down those who'd done him wrong.

Akane got up and checked the condo's refrigerator. Empty but for a bottle of Aloha Shoyu. Nothing in the cupboards but a can of macadamia nuts. He opened it and popped a handful into his mouth while staring out the window at the condo's view of Waikiki Harbor and the ocean beyond. The clang of wind in rigging and the squeak of boats in their moorings made an odd kind of music. A friend of a friend owned this place, and if he hadn't been hungry and bored, he wouldn't have minded being stuck here until he figured out how to get back to the Big Island undetected.

A few minutes later, a coded knock at the door brought Akane to undo the heavy locks to friendlier company than his starchy DA cousin.

Lee Chow, his right-hand man for many years, stood in the doorway with one arm around a brunette, the other around a blonde. "Yo, boss! I brought good times."

"Nice! Go get comfortable, ladies." Akane cocked his head, indicating for the women to enter. The women sashayed past Akane into the front room. He tugged Chow inside, out of earshot, and spoke with his back to them. "What do they know about me?"

Chow's battle-scarred face scrunched in a frown. "The bitches only know that you're an important dude that wants to party."

Akane glanced over at the scantily dressed women, whispering and cooing as they took in the apartment's spectacular downtown view. "Well, they're right about that. I do want to party." He grinned, thinking of the surprises he had in store. "Hope you told them about my alternative tastes."

"Naw, boss. None of my business." Chow kept his gaze down, respectful. The man had never had a clue about Akane's jungle hunting ground outside of Volcano Park, a secret he hadn't shared with anyone but those involved. Having it all come out at trial was humiliating, not something Akane was sure how to turn to his advantage.

But Chow's vote of confidence by bringing the women was promising.

"Thanks, Lee. You can leave now. Go get us some booze, food, bleach, a big sheet of plastic, and some duct tape."

Chow whipped his head up, eyes wide.

Akane guffawed at Chow's stricken expression. "Just kidding. Me and the girls are going to have some fun. Come back soon with enough booze and food, and I might let you join me." He shoved Chow out and shut the door on his lieutenant's worried face.

CHAPTER TWO

THE DANCERS WHIRLED across the stage in perfect unison, the stomp and slide of bare feet on the stage emphasized by a hypnotic Hawaiian chant and the thump of an *ipu* gourd. Fern headdresses gave a feeling of royalty, emphasized by swirling capes of long black hair whirling around their hips. Full skirts, covered with an additional layer of ti leaf, both concealed and enhanced every crisp, defined movement as the dancers told a story through their bodies. Even security specialist Sophie Ang, unfamiliar with hula, could feel the *mana,* Hawaiian spiritual power, vibrating through the performance.

As the action came to a crescendo and ended with the dancers' arms raised high and heads bowed, Sophie's eyes prickled at the beauty and pathos. Watching on the small screen of the phone the client held was mesmerizing; Sophie couldn't imagine how intense it would be to witness such a spectacle up close, in person. "Thank you for showing me that video. It really helps me to understand why the Merrie Monarch Festival is such an important cultural event here in Hilo."

A mixed Hawaiian Asian female who looked approximately

thirty years old, the client wore the kind of fitted floral-print muumuu that indicated a service industry job. A name tag over her left breast spelled out KIM KAUWA. Sophie whisked a price tag off one of a pair of chairs in front of her desk, new since they'd opened the Security Solutions extension office two weeks ago. "Please, come sit down. Can we get you something to drink?"

"No. In fact I can't stay long." Kim's eyes darted nervously to the door, where Sophie's partner Jake Dunn lounged, arms crossed on his chest.

"Jake, come in and join us. Let's all get comfortable. Tell us how we can serve you." Sophie was getting better at the social niceties, though it was still a mental effort to grapple with the mechanics of engaging with others after so many years behind a computer.

Kim took a seat, her purse clutched close. "I looked up your business online. The website said Security Solutions had a brand-new location here on the Big Island, and I just…wondered if you might be able to help me. Us."

"That's what we're here for. Helping people." Jake extended a hand and Kim shook it briefly. Seated, he was still an intimidating sight, his muscular torso packed into a black polo-style Security Solutions logo shirt that left no doubt that he spent a good deal of his free time at the gym.

Jake made small talk with Kim while Sophie scanned the intake form the woman had filled out in the lobby with their receptionist, Felicia.

Kim was thirty-eight years old, lived in Hilo, and worked for the Hawaii Tourism Authority Board as well as Hawaiian Airlines customer service. She was also a volunteer organizer for the famous annual Merrie Monarch Hula Festival that was taking place soon in Hilo. Under "Needs that bring you to us," Kim had listed, *"confidential concerns regarding the Merrie Monarch Festival."*

Sophie looked up and met the woman's dark brown eyes squarely. "Before you get into telling us about the situation that brings you here, and I gather it's sensitive from the way you filled out the form, let me assure you that this initial consultation is completely confidential. We will not disclose anything about your work with our agency to anyone. But perhaps you should know a little bit more about what we do so that you can make an informed decision."

Sophie described the various programs that Security Solutions offered, from the patented artificial intelligence "nanny cam" software installed at high security locations to regular security and alarm monitoring. Bodyguarding, kidnap rescue, and private investigator services were also available, wherein she, Jake, or both, served as private detectives working on behalf of the client or a lawyer.

"That's what I need. Private investigation." Kim knotted her fingers together over her purse. "I'm representing the Hawaii Tourism Authority's Board in this situation. We give a big grant to the Festival every year. I'm also one of the organizers. Well, it seems some of the Festival's money is missing."

Any investigation that could be done online, such as tracking a money trail, was a strength for Sophie, and she exchanged a glance with Jake. "Tell us more."

"It's all very sensitive. The event is so culturally important that even asking questions about something like where the money went… well, I could get plenty of *pilikia*." Kim slipped into pidgin, the Hawaiian creole dialect Sophie was becoming familiar with.

"Don't know *pilikia*, but I get the feeling it's not good," Jake said. "Are you sure you don't want to go to the police with your concern?"

"Oh no. No!" Kim recoiled. "Everybody is related to somebody on this island and has connections—word would get out we're looking into it for sure if I went to the Hilo PD, and we just aren't ready with anything concrete." She took a deep breath, obviously calming herself with an effort. "Let me begin at the beginning. The reason I chose Security Solutions was that you're new in town, and no offense, but you're *haoles*." She looked Sophie up and down, clearly taking her golden-brown skin into consideration. "Outsiders. That's what *haole* means, and that's what I need. A confidential team, with no local networks, to dig into where the money's going."

"How much money are we talking about?" Jake leaned forward, dark brows knit over steely-gray eyes.

"A hundred grand. That's just the Hawaii Tourism Authority's money. There might be more that's missing, I don't know. The Merrie Monarch competition is supported by a lot of bigger businesses such as Hawaiian Airlines. I work for them too and liaise with their charity office to facilitate support of the Festival." Kim coughed a little, hiding her mouth with a hand. "Maybe I need something to drink, after all."

Jake stood up with his usual restless, coiled energy, clearly needing to move. "Let me get you some tea. Sophie, anything?"

"Hot tea would be fine. Thank you."

Jake disappeared. Through the office door, Sophie heard his bantering tone as he spoke with Felicia at her desk.

She met Kim's eyes. "I don't know much about the Merrie Monarch Festival. I will have to research it. As you noticed, it's only been a couple of weeks since we officially opened our doors. But we have all the resources of our parent company on Oahu behind us. Would you like to know a little more?" Kim nodded, and Sophie went on. "I'm a former tech agent with the FBI. I can find most anything online. I love tracking money trails." She cracked her knuckles and rippled her fingers as if using an imaginary keyboard.

This seemed to put Kim more at ease, because the woman smiled. "You both seem...impressive." Her gaze tracked over Sophie, dressed in the black polo shirt and nylon combat pants that she and Jake had decided would be their "uniform" unless they were undercover. "Like you work out a lot."

"We do. Part of the job. We need to be prepared for any sort of emergency. Jake's ex-Special Forces with much investigative experience. And you are right in your assessment. We are outsiders here in Hilo. I'm glad that, for once, it's a strength." Sophie shrugged. "We enjoy using our skills to help people."

"You have an accent. Where are you from?" Kim raised her brows curiously.

"I'm American and Thai. I grew up in Thailand and was educated in Europe. I came to live in the US only five years ago."

Jake returned with Felicia in his wake. The pretty blonde psychology grad student from the University of Hawaii carried a tray with the tea accoutrements on it. She had been sent over from a temp agency Security Solutions had contracted with to help get the agency's satellite office going, and so far, Sophie found her personable and intelligent.

Felicia set the tray, with its mismatched collection of mugs, on the edge of Sophie's desk. "Anything else I can get you?" Her gaze fixed on Jake in mute adoration.

Sophie felt a twinge of something unpleasant tighten her gut. *Felicia must not know she and Jake were involved.* "Thanks, Felicia, that will be all."

The receptionist left, shutting the door behind her, and Jake dealt with the tea until they all had what they wanted. Sophie wrapped her fingers around her hot mug as the beverage steeped, warming her hands. "Kim. Please continue. When and how did you begin to suspect something was wrong with the festival's funding?"

"I helped facilitate the grant to the Festival. I'm not on the Board of Directors, so I don't have access to the financial reports. But the same sponsors were being featured, and the budget is available to organizers to view, and it's the same too. Only this year, PR and advertising aren't nearly at the same level as in the past. Everywhere I turn at the planning meetings I'm hearing that we don't have the money, but I knew the overall budget was similar to last year's."

Jake frowned. "Hmm. You don't have anything more tangible than that?"

Kim looked down at her hands in her lap. "That's why we can't go to the police yet. And when I say 'we' I'm talking about me and my *kumu hula*, Esther Ka`awai."

Sophie jerked, feeling as if she'd been zapped with a red-hot wire. Esther, a well-known Hawaiian wise woman, was Alika Wolcott's grandmother, and Alika was a painful subject to be avoided at all costs. "Isn't Mrs. Ka`awai on Kaua`i?"

"I am studying under her. Esther provides cultural advisory oversight to the event. She was the one to put the pattern together and really bring it to my attention. She is able to do a lot long distance." Kim was oblivious to Sophie's discomfort. "She and I decided to try to get more information without tipping anyone off that we were looking into it."

Sophie squelched apprehension at the thought of interacting with Esther Ka`awai. "Who, exactly, is the client?" Sophie looked down at the application in front of her. "To put it bluntly—who will be paying the bill?"

"The Tourism Authority will be hiring you. I went to them with our concerns, and they gave us a budget." Kim named a figure. "Can you work with that?"

"We certainly can," Jake said. "To start, we will need all the names and contact numbers that you can give us for everyone involved with the Festival."

"I have that on computer. I'll email it to you."

"We should get eyes on the different players and areas involved," Jake went on. "Do you have a plausible way to introduce us, bring us around to meetings and such?"

"Something closest to the truth is always the best," Sophie said. "Jake tends to stand out as a cop or investigator no matter what. Bringing him around as a private security expert to help make sure nothing's stolen or unsafe makes sense. My skills lie behind a computer. I'll be looking for the money trail from the bank. Let's come up with a plan and timetable on how to proceed."

"I'd like us to get started right away," Kim said. "The Festival is in a month, and the sooner we find out where the money went, the sooner we can get the funds back and put them to work to make this the best event ever." Her brown eyes shone almost feverishly. "We owe it to everyone who gives so much to make this event the magnificent cultural event it is."

CHAPTER THREE

SEATED on the top step of his front porch, Terence Chang surveyed the Chang family's former compound. Terence was proud of how neat the place looked now: he'd removed the many junked cars, the rusting freezer, and the pile of barrels his cousins had stored meth-making chemicals in. His two brindled pit bulls wandered and sniffed around the yard, marking their favorite spots.

Terence sipped his coffee. He liked it black, and fresh, made from one hundred percent Kona beans grown on his own plantation, one of his several legit businesses. He let the fragrant brew roll around on his tongue and settle on his palate, as he gazed down at the expensive black basketball shoes that were one of his few indulgences.

He had tried hard to go straight.

He had made many good changes. He'd gone to college. Built up his own businesses and run interference for the family via computers and managing the Chang family's legal affairs. Until his cousin Byron, head of the family, had been gunned down, that peripheral role had been enough. It hadn't been long since the brutal slaying, but the Chang empire already seemed to be coming apart at the seams since Terence's psycho cousin Akane had escaped just after his trial.

There were those in the family who thought Akane should take over in the vacuum left by Byron's death—that his brutality and bloodthirstiness were signs of strength.

Terence knew better.

He sipped, trying to regain the simple pleasure the beverage had given him only moments ago.

She had liked his coffee, too.

He refused to let her name arise in his mind—but it did anyway. *Julie Weathersby.* His own personal Kryptonite.

Julie's face filled his memory: her wide blue eyes, happy smile, those pale freckles on her nose. The little sounds she made in his arms. The way she snuggled into him, trusting as a puppy.

He'd never been anyone's hero before.

Terence tightened his mouth bitterly. The coffee tasted like ash.

He'd rescued Julie—picked her up on a deserted road, running for her life from Akane. He'd prevented that brutal rapist batshit crazy serial killer from tearing Julie apart, emotionally and physically.

What he hadn't counted on was falling for the girl.

Hadn't counted on letting himself hope he could have some other kind of life and share it with someone special.

But he couldn't have her. Or that life. Because the worst thing that could happen to the Changs, and everyone around them, would be for Akane to take over the business.

Akane had friends who owed him. Side hustles no one knew anything about. And if Terence didn't step up to take Byron's place, there was a very good chance Akane would come out of left field, waste anyone who offered competition, and bring on a reign of blood like the Changs hadn't been through since the thirties, when they'd warred with the Chinese triads for power and come out on top.

The phone rang on the step beside him, and his dogs looked up, pricking their ears. Terence read the ID window: *Hilo PD.* "Terence Chang here."

Nowhere to hide. No point in trying.

"This is Detective Freitan from Hilo PD. Your cousin's crime scene has been released. I suggest you contact a cleaning service that specializes in biohazard cleanup and blood removal before you go back onto the premises."

Freitan was a badass mofo of a female detective. His balls crawled for cover whenever he had the misfortune of dealing with her. "Thanks for the call, Detective. What can you tell me about efforts to capture my deranged murderer cousin?" *No sense glossing over the truth.*

"Not my case, Mr. Chang. His capture is an FBI matter. I'm sure someone will be in touch with you soon to find out possible locations where your dear family member might hide." Freitan sounded hard, flippant.

Terence took another sip of coffee to wet his throat. "I appreciate any support Hilo PD can give me in capturing Akane. Believe me when I tell you, we don't want him around here."

"I heard you were going straight, Chang. But you sound like you're speaking for the family on this matter." Freitan's tone was serious.

"I'm speaking for the family on this, yes." Time to "shit or get off the pot," as his beloved but terrifying *tutu*, Healani, had always said. It couldn't hurt to establish his authority with the local PD early on.

"Your concern about Akane's capture is noted," Freitan replied. "I'll let the FBI know that you are their official point of contact."

"You do that." Terence ended the call with a punch of his thumb.

He had a lot of arrangements to make, starting with getting in cleaners to remove all trace of the carnage of Byron's murder. He needed to get the downtown warehouse space ready for a big meeting, and there was no time to waste.

Terence went back into the house, already working his phone.

The dogs trailed him as he walked through the redone living room with its spare, modern décor.

He wasn't going to get the girl or the life he'd hoped for. But he had inherited the office that had been Byron's, and his father's, and his grandfather's—and maybe, just maybe, he could eventually steer the Chang empire in a different direction.

First, he had to step up and take over, and even that wasn't going to be easy.

CHAPTER FOUR

Jake trailed Ando Bautista, the coverall-clad site manager, through the Edith Kanaka`ole Tennis Stadium where the Merrie Monarch Festival was scheduled to be held. Kim had brought him to the multipurpose convex building after their initial meeting and had taken him straight to the property manager's office. They'd run into several people associated with the Festival there, including the event manager, Ilima Cruz, a majestic Hawaiian woman with considerable presence. Kim had introduced Jake as a "security expert hired by the Tourism Authority Board to make sure the auditorium met safety standards."

So far, that cover was working. Bautista, a grizzled Filipino of unknown age, had whisked him off to tour the building. Enjoying a chance to talk about his passion, Bautista waxed expansive about his years at the building and the various challenges to setting up events. His pidgin was so thick Jake had to strain to understand.

"Back in the day when the Merrie Monarch first came heah, was small kine. We built a stage with volunteers. Now, the event so big, we gotta build plenty seating to hold 'em all, and it sell out right away. If we had one bigger place in Hilo, we would fill that too."

Jake paused, hands on hips, surveying the dim, cavernous area, its interior floodlights off. He perused the well-marked tennis court in the center. "I've seen video. This place gets packed. I'm not concerned just with the structural safety aspects; in fact, I'm less worried about that. I'm here mostly for personal safety and crime prevention. Can you tell me about any incidents that might have happened over the years?"

"Oh, we get plenny support from the Hilo PD. Off-duty officers direct traffic, provide security. No worries there." Bautista gestured. "Only place get small kine *pilikia* was the bat'rooms. Come see."

"*Pilikia*. I keep hearing that word."

"Trouble," Bautista said. "Some folks, they like fo' drink or use drugs in the bat'rooms. We get one camera over the door for the event in case we need fo' see who went in or out. If we get funding for it, one police officer stands outside, too."

Jake leaped on this opportunity to explore the situation that had triggered the case. "Funding? I heard things are tight this year." He touched Bautista's arm, deciding to take a chance on the voluble little man. "Don't say anything, but part of why I was hired was to check into what's been happening with this year's Festival money."

"You know, I'm just the building manager. I nevah know notting," Bautista said loudly. He glanced back and forth theatrically, then gestured for Jake to follow. Over near a row of closed garbage receptacles, the building manager leaned close. "I been hearing those guys running the marketing and ads been helping themselves to some of the budget supposed to go to the Festival. My cuz, she one cleaner at the office. She wen' tell me she think something smell funny cuz never been no ads this year like in the past. Usually the trash cans, they full of all the lists and sketches. This year, hardly notting. Only one big sign near the airport, where everyone going see 'em."

"Thanks, Mr. Bautista." Jake noted the agency's name and took another chance and slipped a rolled fifty-dollar bill into the man's hand, along with his card. "You are helping the Festival by helping me. Anything else you come across, give me a call."

"I do dat." Bautista nodded, slipping his hand into the pocket of his coveralls.

Jake returned to the building's main office and glanced at the wall clock over the property manager's desk. Almost five p.m., and the place would soon close. He glanced around. "Is Ms. Cruz still available?"

"No, she had just stopped by to check in on some Festival business," the clerk manning the phones said. "But she leaves a number with us in case of need." The girl provided that to Jake.

Jake was already dialing as he headed through the building toward the white Security Solutions SUV, currently in 'stealth mode,' the magnetic signage touting their services that could be put up on the doors stowed in the vehicle's storage area. "Ms. Cruz? This is Jake Dunn with Security Solutions. We met briefly at the stadium. Can I get a meeting with you to discuss the security planning for the event?"

"Sure. I was just leaving. Are you still here at the Stadium?"

"I'm in the parking lot."

"Me too." Cruz got out of a maroon minivan parked at the other end of the lot and waved, and Jake grinned as he walked toward her.

"Thanks for taking the time to talk right now. Saves me another trip."

"Sure. Why don't you get into the van? We can chat in comfort." Cruz clicked her door unlocked and cleared a stuffed toy off the front seat. "Sorry about the mess."

Jake hopped in. "Sorry for invading your personal vehicle with company business."

"Speaking of. What is this security planning you're doing, and why is the Tourism Authority involved?" Cruz had large, intelligent dark eyes, and a frown line that seemed chiseled between her brows, as if she were used to being skeptical.

Sophie had run a preliminary background check on the woman before Jake left the office, and she was squeaky clean—not even a parking ticket, and Kim had sworn Cruz was on the up and up. "Our firm has been hired to look into possible misuse of Tourism Authority funds."

"Oh no!" Cruz clapped a hand over her mouth. "This can't get out. It would ruin our reputation!"

Jake made a settling gesture with his hand. "It's early days yet. We're just getting started looking into things, and we have no intention of ruining anything. The interested parties just want to make sure that all funds designated for different areas of the Festival are accounted for."

"Absolutely. I understand." Cruz nodded. "But please keep this investigation confidential."

"I probably shouldn't even have told you." Jake smiled as boyishly as he could, hoping to disarm the woman. "We hope we're wrong, that we can find the funds. But if not, we'll handle everything discreetly. We do Security Solutions no favors incurring the wrath of our clients and any organizations we're working for, directly or indirectly."

Cruz seemed to relax a little. She picked up an insulated water bottle from a nearby cup holder and took a sip. "Can you tell me who your client is?"

"I'm afraid not. But it would help us greatly if you, as the program director, could tell us if you have any concerns."

"I'm sorry, but I'm a little out of touch with the nuts and bolts, to be honest." Sun pouring in through the windshield had begun to heat the interior; Jake lowered his window as Cruz slid on a pair of sunglasses and turned on the car to get the air conditioning going. "There's a committee in charge of PR and budget. I attend their meetings, but my focus has been on the competition aspect—making sure that everyone has a fair chance to qualify for the competition, and that the judging is unbiased."

"I'm sure you've got your work cut out for you. Do you rely on Esther Ka'awai to help advise you?" Jake was curious about Alika's grandmother and her involvement.

"Esther is a treasure, but she's more for making sure the overall cultural integrity of the Festival is preserved, and that we observe Hawaiian best practices in how we put everything together." Cruz's arched brows drew together. "I think our main spend, other than the rental of the actual facility and staff, is on the media and PR for the event."

Jake nodded. "Thanks. I just wanted to get your take on things. Please keep this probe confidential."

She inclined her head. "Of course. I appreciate your keeping it confidential, as well. Last thing we need is negative talk in the community."

Jake opened his door and got out. "I'm all for staying out of trouble!"

Cruz tilted her head with a smile. "You might be in the wrong business for that, Mr. Dunn. Good luck and good hunting."

Mission accomplished so far, Jake headed for the Banyan Tree Motel, a run-down local establishment nestled in the curve of Hilo Bay where he and Sophie had been staying until they located something more permanent.

Sophie still insisted on separate rooms in spite of spending nights together, but he didn't argue. The lady needed her psychological space, and it behooved him to give it to her.

Jake's pulse picked up as he anticipated being alone with Sophie at the end of the day. She had sent him off with Kim to tour the stadium, telling him she had computer work to do and an appointment to go to outside the office.

That appointment had to be with Dr. Wilson, and he was glad she was going. Sophie wasn't sleeping well in spite of the number of orgasms he made sure she achieved nightly. She'd drop off to sleep, but later spend hours tossing and turning, caught in dark dreams. Sometimes she woke with a cry, or lay still, weeping silently—and he could always tell when she did, though she tried to hide it from him.

And no matter how many times he asked what was bothering her, she wouldn't tell him.

But Jake was no idiot.

Sophie was torturing herself over a recent attempt on her life and its aftermath. A small explosive device in a package rigged to blow had damaged her ribs and given her a concussion—but her former boyfriend Alika, who'd met Sophie in her father's lobby and picked up the bomb, had been the one to take real damage. The real estate developer had lost his arm and been in ICU for the better part of a week. He was finally out of the hospital and had been transported back to his home on Kaua`i.

Jake had been monitoring the situation via Marcella, Sophie's best friend, and it seemed like Alika was recovering as best as could be expected. Sophie had refused to see or communicate with the man, though, and Jake guessed that she was eaten up with guilt for indirectly causing Alika's mutilation. It was as if, in cutting Alika off, she'd increased her attachment to him.

Jake scowled, navigating the busy downtown Hilo traffic. He'd thought he won the lottery the day Sophie asked him to be her lover. He'd been crazy for her—emotionally, physically, in every way possible. He'd been sure there was no wall she could put up against him that he couldn't break down, at least physically.

And at first, that part of their relationship had been amazing. Sophie sought him out every night. She initiated the sex, and it was hot as hell. She was aggressive, responsive, as hungry as he was. They made love until exhaustion took them both over.

But then, the dreams. The insomnia and crying. Sophie had stopped looking him in the eye when they made love. Jake felt a distance widening between them no matter their physical pleasure, and even that had begun to feel empty as she withdrew deeper into herself.

He hated the secrets. The lies. The *others* that lay between them, unspoken and unacknowledged.

He pulled up at the motel. *Maybe they'd have a breakthrough tonight.* Sophie had told him she'd meet him at seven at a seafood place they both liked, the first time they hadn't just called for some kind of takeout and proceeded to the sex part of the evening.

Since he'd arrived first, Jake unlocked Sophie's room and let Ginger and Tank out. The friendly, affectionate Lab and his rescue pit bull got walked in the morning before they left for work, once at noon by whomever was free, and in the evening when either of them arrived back at the motel.

Seeing Jake, Ginger woofed in joy as if she'd been abandoned forever. The Lab flung herself on her back at his feet, begging with her whole body for a tummy rub, while Tank looked on, tongue lolling.

If only Sophie was half as in love with Jake as her dog was.

CHAPTER FIVE

SHELDON HAMILTON, CEO of Security Solutions, aka Connor, watched Sophie out of the corner of his eye. He'd flown all the way back from his island in Thailand for this meeting, and the flare of excitement at seeing Sophie again had already been extinguished by worry and disappointment.

They sat in his office area on board the corporate jet parked in Hilo Airport, and waited for the video conferencing software to contact Agent McDonald of the CIA. They'd have total privacy on the plane: no interruptions, uninvited guests, or security breaches.

Sophie's full mouth was pinched, her honey-brown eyes shadowed. She'd always reminded him of a golden eagle, wild and hard to tame. It was a miracle that she'd ever flown with him and told him she loved him. He couldn't have ruined his chances with her permanently. *No.* He would win her back. With patience. With time. With relentless will and unstoppable love. With all the ways he could help and serve her that no one else could. She'd said she forgave him for that terrible mistake he'd made; it was a start. "You don't look like you've been resting well."

"I haven't been." Her eyes stayed down, fixed on the computer tablet she held.

Connor's imagination went in a bad place. His gut knotted. "Not even with Jake in your bed?"

"Not even with Jake." Sophie still refused to meet his gaze. She was so honest and literal.

There was no more time for that line of conversation because the little icon stopped spinning on the laptop's monitor.

CIA Agent McDonald's jowly, florid face filled the screen. "Mr. Hamilton. And Sophie Ang. How's the new operation going in Hilo?"

"We're done setting up and have our first cases," Sophie replied. "Security Solutions is officially open for business in Hilo."

McDonald's bushy brows snapped together. "I thought that extension office was just a cover for you, Ms. Ang."

"Rather expensive cover for Security Solutions to create an entire branch office for one woman, working for nothing for the CIA," Connor said drily. "Ms. Ang is our employee and has actual duties to perform."

McDonald's color grew deeper. The man definitely had a blood pressure problem. "Have you had enough time to think over our proposal?"

"And what is that, exactly? Spell it out for us," Connor said.

"The proposal was not to you, Hamilton, nor to Security Solutions." McDonald turned his gaze to Sophie. "Ms. Ang. It's disappointing that you feel you needed to hide behind your employer when we offered you, and you alone, an opportunity to go after your mother's organization, the Yām Khûmkan. We offered training. A cover. A support system. A chance to prove your patriotism. Maybe get a little revenge." He bounced his brows suggestively.

"I will be honest with you, Agent McDonald, in the spirit of full disclosure—and because you are likely monitoring me and know all of this anyway." Sophie spoke precisely. "I have been struggling with depression, in no small part triggered by discovering that my mother, who I thought was an invalid, has actually, for my entire life, been a spy. She married my father and had a child as cover.

She sold me to a sadistic husband in return for favors to her clandestine organization." Sophie spread her long, tawny fingers wide on the tabletop as if seeking to ground herself. "Anyone might find these revelations a little upsetting, but for me, combined with a series of traumatic events…I have not been myself." She gave a small, bitter laugh that hurt Connor to hear. "Whoever that 'self' is. I am not mentally and emotionally fit to be a double agent for the CIA right now. And for the record, I don't need to prove my patriotism."

McDonald's cheeks puffed indignantly as he drew breath for a rebuttal, but Connor cut him off with a hand gesture. "Sophie is available only in the capacity which I described to you when I made contact last week: as an employee of Security Solutions. I will continue to be involved in this project every step of the way. Your office should have received our contract by now. We will be charging fair market value for investigation services of this sensitive and specialized nature."

McDonald held up a paper. "Our office got the fax. This is highly irregular. We have many confidential assets throughout the world, and we set the terms, thank you very much."

"Not this time." Connor let some of his anger show in a hard and steady gaze. "Ms. Ang is not going anywhere or doing anything alone."

Sophie touched Connor's arm out of sight of the camera. Gratitude was conveyed in the soft squeeze of her hand, warm and intimate—and over too soon.

McDonald blew out a gusty sigh and threw up his hands. "I'll take this back to my people. They aren't going to be happy."

"Take it or leave it." Connor said. "We have plenty of work for Ms. Ang without complicating things further."

"You might want to make nice with the CIA, Mr. Hamilton, or you might find access to your private island in Thailand getting a little tricky," McDonald growled.

"Are you threatening me?" Connor smiled without humor. *He'd love to unleash the Ghost to find some dirt on McDonald.* Taking on the CIA was a challenge he'd relish.

This time, Sophie's hand touching his arm was a restraining pressure.

She didn't want him to go after this guy, or the CIA. She probably still had some childish fantasy of finding a way to redeem her conscienceless harpy of a mother and didn't want Connor to endanger that.

McDonald shook his head. "We're getting off on the wrong foot. I will take this contract to my superiors. In the meantime, if you could cozy up to Pim Wat and her organization while you're going to therapy for your depression, Ms. Ang, your country would be grateful." McDonald managed to sound both sarcastic and sincere. "And in the interest of bringing useful information to the table, I've got some news as well. Akane Chang has escaped. You might want to take extra precautions."

The man reached out, pushed a button, and the screen went black.

CHAPTER SIX

S<small>OPHIE RUBBED</small> the scar on her cheekbone. Touching the rough, bumpy ridge, oddly numb and sometimes tingly, had become something of a habit. A gunshot wound repair, the skin graft over a prosthetic cheekbone had altered her appearance, but Sophie was the one who seemed most bothered by it. She breathed deliberately—her injured ribs still hurt, and McDonald's revelation had made her want to get up and run. Or fight. Or both.

Akane Chang was, apparently, a nightmare she hadn't yet left behind.

Connor stared at her intensely, sea-blue eyes hidden behind those dark contacts and hipster glasses that were part of his Sheldon Hamilton disguise.

"You knew about Akane Chang." Sophie made herself stop rubbing the scar.

"I monitor everything that might be a threat." Connor removed the glasses and leaned forward to take out the contacts, slipping the lenses into a small plastic container. "I was looking forward to this occasion of privacy to discuss his escape."

"I stopped monitoring Akane after the trial," Sophie said. "Was just hoping that monster was going to be behind bars and out of circulation permanently. *Son of a pox-ridden whore!*" She swore in Thai and closed her eyes for a moment, covering them with a hand. "Couldn't just one sadistic killer I've dealt with stay in jail?"

As Connor had pointed out, she hadn't been sleeping well. She and Jake had been staying in a run-down motel in Hilo Bay, and in spite of a lot of very good sex, insomnia plagued her nightly, peppered with trauma flashbacks and feedback loops of regret, many of which involved Alika Wolcott.

"That's the depression talking." Dr. Wilson, her therapist, spoke in her head. "Guilt doesn't help anyone."

Yes. The depression had a voice, a tone even.

Fortunately, she had a session with Dr. Wilson soon. There would be a lot to cover.

Connor rapped his knuckles on the table to get her attention. "We have a reprieve from the CIA situation for the moment, but your mother needs something to keep her on the line. I propose we call her; you can tell her about Akane."

"Why would I do that?"

Connor shrugged. "She is an assassin, after all."

Sophie really focused on Connor's face for the first time that day. The man was almost too handsome with his classical features, square jaw, and those changeable blue-green eyes. His dark brown hair was a part of his Hamilton persona, but she still remembered it blond.

She stiffened at the reminder that Pim Wat was not only a spy— her mother was a murderer. "I only have your word on that."

Connor's eyes flashed with temper. "Why don't you ask Pim Wat yourself?" He grabbed Sophie's phone, scrolled a moment and pressed a button, put it on speaker, and pushed the device toward Sophie.

No time to prepare, rehearse, or otherwise brace herself.

Pim Wat's husky voice came on, speaking Thai. "Sophie Malee?"

"Mother." Sophie blew out a breath, not sure how to proceed.

"You took long enough to call. I was beginning to be concerned." Pim Wat sounded sad, a tone Sophie was all too familiar with—and that note sparked anger. *Because it was fake, that sadness, a lie.* Sophie had dealt with it her entire childhood.

"Quit pretending, Mother. You just want to know if I'll do your job."

A pause.

"You're testy today." Pim Wat's voice had modulated upward. They were still speaking Thai, and Sophie slanted a glance at Connor, not sure if he was following everything—or if he needed to. His head was cocked to the side, and he gave a slight nod. He'd been studying Thai, and he was following so far.

"Perhaps that new lover of yours is not so good in bed," Pim Wat mused.

Sophie flushed. "You're spying on me now?"

"It's what I do, Sophie Malee." Pim Wat's voice was coolly amused. Only her mother called her that. "Jake Dunn appears to be a fine physical specimen. I'm sure I could teach him whatever he might be lacking in skills."

"By Kali's left tit, Mother, this is no way to get on my good side," Sophie said.

"You and your varied deity curses. Amusing. I need to placate you now? Very well." Pim Wat sighed, put upon. "I killed the man who tried to blow you up with the bomb. It was not easy. I took a bullet to do it. In the vest, it's true, but it still hurt like a water buffalo's kick. And I did that for you, Sophie."

Sophie opened and closed her mouth, meeting Connor's gaze. *Her mother was bragging about a kill!*

Connor closed one eye in a slow, deliberate wink.

That wink that told her she wasn't alone.

That wink that reassured her they were on the same side—and it was not her mother's.

And that wink that hinted at a deeper knowledge of everything about the situation.

Trust Connor to be way out in front of Pim Wat. Sophie didn't have to know exactly what he was doing to know that it would be effective.

Sophie felt ridiculously reassured. *Connor could handle her mother.* She looked back down at the phone, trying to muster an appropriate response.

Pim Wat went on, apparently concerned about Sophie's silence. "The Lizard was a cagey and cautious assassin. He wouldn't have stopped trying to tick you off his kill list—he was egotistical that way." Pim Wat sounded primly disapproving. "So, I removed him."

"You're a killer as well as a spy?" Sophie didn't have to fake the way her voice cracked. "My mother. A lying murderer."

"Oh, silly girl," Pim Wat snapped. "You and your American self-pity, tender sensibilities and mental anguish. *Please.* Spare me the petty judgments. I do what needs to be done. What others cannot. For the good of my country and my family." Sophie was chilled at the similarity of Pim Wat's words to things the Ghost had said. "If you cannot see what I did as the gift it was, you are the petty one."

Sophie shut her eyes, trying to sort through her responses to find one that would serve the purpose of engaging her mother and building trust.

"The Lizard was nearly effective at killing me several times. The world is a better place without him," Sophie said. *That much was true.* "If only Akane Chang could meet the same fate. The man escaped from jail on Oahu."

Pim Wat cursed, a fluid rush of profanity that put Sophie's creative attempts to shame. "Akane Chang is dangerous to you, my daughter."

"No shit." The Americanism seemed appropriate. Sophie met Connor's gaze again. "I'm worried about Akane being on the loose. The Big Island is his home. He will be coming here."

"Where was he last seen?"

"I don't know anything but what I've told you. His escape is being kept quiet."

A long pause. "When can we meet in person, to discuss your role with the Yām Khûmkạn?"

"Soon, Mother. Just give me a little more time to get situated. I'm looking for a more permanent dwelling, and getting the office up and running…"

"All of that is irrelevant. I want you to get started on the computer system rebuild that our organization needs," Pim Wat snapped.

"I'm telling you, I'm not ready. Find someone else if you need it done right away," Sophie said.

"Perhaps I will." Pim Wat ended the call with a click.

Sophie sagged in her chair, covering her face with her hands. *"Devil swine! Foul stench of a bloated corpse! Rat-infested warehouse filled with broken dildos!"*

"Not bad, but I rather think your mother has you beat in the cursing department," Connor observed. "Still wondering whether or not she's an assassin?"

"No. She definitely confirmed it." Sophie put her hands down, glancing at the phone. "Oh no! I have to meet Jake soon. We're having dinner in town."

Connor's expression didn't change—it just seemed to freeze. "Have fun." He got up from the table and turned his back, sliding his laptop into a briefcase. "I'll be here in Hilo for a few more hours. Going to Oahu to check in with Bix and the main office. There are company matters that demand Sheldon Hamilton's attention."

"I want to bring Jake in on this." Sophie spread her hands on the table, steadying herself. "He deserves it."

"This?"

"This. He already knows about my mother. I want him to know everything about what's going on. You. The Yām Khûmkạn."

"No."

"No? You don't get to dictate everything about this situation!" Sophie stood. "These things affect me. They're my life. I don't want to keep secrets from Jake that I don't have to!"

"Trouble in paradise?" Connor quirked a brow. "Jake wants to be more than your booty call?"

"Oh." Sophie sucked a breath. "I'm done here." She swept up her nylon pack and headed for the door of the jet, pushed it open.

Connor touched her arm. "Sophie. I'm sorry. That was rude."

"Yes, it was." She glared at him. "You're jealous."

He stiffened. "I'm doing my best."

They stared at each other for a long moment.

Sophie finally sighed. "I won't tell him about you and the Ghost. But please. All this sneaking around with the Yām Khûmkạn and the CIA would be so much easier if I didn't have to hide everything. He's suspicious. And he's jealous, too." Sophie took a step down out of the plane. Warm wind, smelling of diesel fumes, swirled around her. She glanced out at the bulk of Kilauea. The wind direction had changed, a rare occurrence, and brought volcanic emissions, commonly known as vog, with it. The soft gray of the particulate ash shrouded Hilo like a photographer's filter.

"Damn it." Connor tugged at his hair in agitation. "Tell him if you must. But keep me out of it. We'll talk soon."

CHAPTER SEVEN

SOPHIE SHOOK out her napkin and laid it over her lap in the candlelit dining room of the Hilo Bay Seafood Cafe. She wished that she'd had time to go home and change into something other than the Security Solutions uniform. Jake had; his dark hair was still damp with comb tracks, and he smelled of the lemony aftershave she'd come to love. A silk button-down in midnight blue enhanced his muscular form and brought out the ring of blue in his remarkable gray eyes.

Those eyes seemed to glow in the candlelight as he handed her a glass of wine. "I took the liberty of ordering you something since you were a little late."

Sophie nodded, sipping the beverage. "This is good. What is it?"

"A nice little moscato. I notice you like things sweet."

"And I like how you notice what I like."

They smiled at each other.

Jake brought his glass of red to chime with Sophie's in a gentle toast. "To our first official date out in public as a couple."

Heat suffused Sophie's chest as she remembered Connor's barb about Jake being her "booty call." She thrust the memory away and sipped, mind scrabbling over how to proceed with the conversation.

Mercifully, the waiter arrived to regale them with dinner specials.

They ordered, and after he left, Sophie took a hefty sip of wine for courage. "Jake. I have something to tell you."

"Where you were this afternoon?" Jake quirked a dark brow. His attempt at a humorous tone fell flat; Sophie could hear the grit behind it.

"I was meeting Sheldon Hamilton. We are working on a project."

"Ah. Our mysterious CEO. That makes sense."

Sophie wasn't imagining the way Jake's shoulders loosened in relief. He didn't know about the Ghost, didn't have any reason to be jealous of Hamilton—*and that was a good thing.*

"Hamilton has been helping me navigate things with my mother. You see, Pim Wat didn't just reappear in my life to resume a relationship. She had a proposal: that I join her clandestine organization, the Yām Khûmkạn, and provide them with tech support."

Jake's eyes widened. "No wonder you've been sleeping badly!" He reached over to cover her cold hands with his warm ones. "Ah, God, Sophie. That woman. Such a bitch! You deserve a mom who loves and appreciates you."

He had no idea how really horrible Pim Wat was. Sophie blinked quick tears away, looking down at their joined hands. Jake's instant, unstinting compassion undid her—and she was only telling him a piece of the truth. The worm of guilt turned in her guts. She couldn't swallow past the lump in her throat.

"Come here." Jake tugged at her hands. "Come sit with me."

They were in an old-fashioned leatherette booth; she felt silly, but sitting next to him wasn't impossible. Sophie slid around the booth until she was flush against Jake's warm, hard bulk, but that wasn't enough for him.

Jake hauled Sophie into his lap, wedging them in tight behind the curve of the table. He snuggled her close, tucking her under his chin and wrapping his thick arms around her. "I wish I could kick her ass," he whispered in her ear. "I hate her for hurting you."

She hid her face in his shirt as Jake kissed her hair and rocked her close. *She didn't deserve the love he showered on her so gener-*

ously. Thinking about it almost made her burst into tears, and she breathed deep and even to keep from crying openly.

She heard the waiter return. Jake directed the man to leave the plates, and Sophie finally lifted her head when he'd gone. "I'm sorry for not telling you sooner. Hamilton just gave me the okay." *Such a pale shadow of the truth.*

"I'm so glad to finally know what's been going on with you." The relief in Jake's expression almost broke her heart. "Tell me more."

"We're working with the CIA. They want me to penetrate the Yām Khûmkạn. Hamilton's using my job at Security Solutions to protect me from both factions. I'm going into my mother's organization, but I won't be alone."

"I have to hear everything about this. But I'll be honest." Jake blew out a breath that tickled her ear. "I was worried it was something worse."

"Like what?" Sophie eased out of Jake's lap to sit beside him.

Jake pushed her plate in front of her. "Like…Alika." Jake had his eyes on his plate now. They ate side by side in silence for a few minutes. Sophie couldn't taste a thing.

"Alika is still a problem," Sophie said softly. "I feel terrible about what happened to him. So guilty. And I'm having flashbacks to the explosion almost every night."

"I thought you were talking to Dr. Wilson today," Jake said. "That's where I thought you went this afternoon."

"I see her tomorrow. I hope she can help me." Sophie shoved another bite into her mouth and chewed mechanically. "It's been hard. Keeping so many secrets from you."

Jake had only taken a few bites of his dinner, but he thrust the plate aside. His gray eyes gleamed silver in the candlelight. "Finally, you're telling me what I've needed to know—what's really been going on with you. Let's get out of here." He gripped her hand, and the touch lit a fire in her belly. "I need to be with you. Alone. Now."

CHAPTER EIGHT

SOPHIE'S HEART was still pounding from their lovemaking as she rested her head on Jake's chest. The deep thunder of his pulse filled her ear. Cool night air wafted over them, wicking away the sweat of passion.

The bedside lamp was on. Sophie enjoyed the sight of her tawny skin against Jake's paler, tanned bulk as she stroked his chest and abs. The visual of her long fingers playing with the arrow of hair that pointed toward his narrow hips was entrancing. She slid her slim, smooth leg up and down his muscular, hairy one, liking the textures, the feel of his heat beneath her coolness.

"All the ways we're different is so sexy," Sophie murmured.

Jake didn't reply, and she sneaked a peek at his face.

Sleeping, his solid jaw had relaxed. Those riveting gray eyes were closed, leaving a fan of black lashes resting on high cheekbones. A snore rumbled in his chest, puffing past lips made soft and pink from kissing.

He was adorable.

Well, too big and rugged to be adorable.

But still...so *lovable.* Did she love him? *He deserved it.*

Sophie traced the knot of a bullet hole in his shoulder. She'd been present for that one and the memory of it still made her stomach tighten. Her fingers slid over the various scars and scrapes left on his skin by a lifetime spent in vigorous, dangerous activities.

Jake wasn't a deeply complex or spiritual man. He was a physical one, and he expressed his love, and all of his passions, with his body.

In many ways they *were* different. But in this one, the same.

She slept, and this time, didn't dream.

Day Two

THE NEXT MORNING, Sophie watched as Dr. Wilson settled herself in the overstuffed lounger she favored, a tablet on her knee and stylus poised. "It's been way too long, Sophie."

"I know." Seated across from the psychologist on a low leather couch, Sophie shook her head. "I can't believe I haven't seen you since before the Akane Chang trial."

"We're in agreement then. No matter what's happening in your life, you'll make the time to come for counseling." Wearing a wrap dress in a floral print, kitten-heeled sandals, and a casual blonde bob, the psychologist looked younger than her fifty-something years. Her keenly intelligent blue eyes searched Sophie's face. "Something good happened recently?"

"Multiple orgasms." Sophie's neck and chest felt hot. "Jake and I are together. Officially."

Dr. Wilson laughed. "Sophie, I never cease to be surprised at the things you say. Never stop being you. We'll get to the orgasms later, but for now, I'd like to review your current symptoms and situation."

Sophie had contacted Dr. Wilson the minute the recent Akane Chang trial on Oahu was over, trying to get an appointment, but they'd both been busy—Sophie with setting up the new Security Solutions office, and Dr. Wilson with other clients. Dr. Wilson had recommended an app for Sophie to use to track her mental state: a checklist on mood, physical feelings and symptoms, sleep, activity, and eating patterns.

Sophie took out her phone. "I'll send this data to you from the app now."

She forwarded it, and Dr. Wilson studied the graph on her phone. "Hmm. Looks like sleep has been a problem. Volatile affect. Stomach trouble. And overall your mood is still low. I'd say depression is being complicated by some PTSD symptoms."

"Exactly. I keep dreaming about the bomb going off." Sophie shut her eyes. She could clearly see her father's apartment building's swanky lobby where things had gone so badly wrong.

"Talk it through with me. Maybe lie down if that helps."

"I don't think I can lie down." Sophie rubbed the scar on her cheekbone. She took a deep breath and blew it out, focusing to remember the series of events. "Connor brought me to the building the day before the trial. He said he'd called Hazel Matsue, the marshal I was working with on the case, to meet us there. I told him I didn't think that was necessary; the building had security." Sophie shook her head. "How wrong I was. I was dressed in my Mary Watson identity as I went in. Ginger was excited, recognizing a familiar place. The security guard was an old man I didn't know. He told me I had a visitor." Sophie shut her eyes. "I thought it was Matsue. The visitor was seated in a chair behind a decorative palm." The story flowed out of her with her eyes closed, like seeing a movie in slow motion. "The visitor was Alika."

Dr. Wilson sucked in a soft breath. "Oh my God."

"Yes. I was surprised to see him. I had left him no contact information after a night we spent together in his hotel room in Hilo." Sophie put the tips of her fingers over her eyes, holding onto darkness. "Alika seemed…different. He was dressed up and looked very handsome. Wanted to talk to me alone."

"What was his demeanor like?" Dr. Wilson's voice drew her deeper into the memory.

"He was nervous, I think. But trying not to seem that way.

Alika's always so calm and in control of himself. But he seemed… very determined about something. He showed his desire for me with just a few words." Sophie felt the heat of tears filling her eyes. Wetness slid out from under her fingertips and down her cheeks. "Before we went up in the elevator the security guard told me that I had a package." She stopped, struggling to keep her breath even, struggling to keep the tears from taking over.

"Go on, Sophie. You can do this. You need to tell this story to let its poison out."

"Yes." Sophie lowered her hands and blinked at Dr. Wilson, who handed her a box of tissues. "I'd slept with Alika the last time I saw him. We'd been shot at. I was hiding in his room from the killer. It was just the one time, but it changed things between us. Deepened things. We had not been intimate in all our years of knowing each other before that. But a lot of my depression and suicidal thoughts on the lava field were because I'd cut him off, for his own good, because my life is too dangerous for a civilian like him. And all that said, surprised as I was by his turning up in the lobby, I was happy to see him." Sophie pressed a wad of tissues to her face. "I was trying not to feel all of that. Trying to remember I was still in danger. When the guard said I had a package, I was cognizant enough to stop and ask who it was from." Sophie took a deep, steadying breath and met Dr. Wilson's eyes. "He said it was from you."

"What?" Dr. Wilson recoiled, a hand coming up to her throat. "No!"

"Yes. And the box was addressed to Mary Watson, so I thought it must be legitimate. You knew about that identity. You knew I would likely be going to my father's apartment at some point. I thought the package was some therapy supplies, books or something. Ginger was making a fuss, trying to smell it. Alika took the box and walked to the elevator. 'I'll carry this for the lady,' he said."

"Oh, Sophie, I'm just sick that my name was used to gain your trust!" Dr. Wilson's face had gone pale. "Oh no!"

Sophie continued woodenly. "I followed Alika toward the elevator, but Ginger wanted to smell the potted palm and tugged me aside. Alika was standing in the doorway reaching for the button. I was walking toward him, with Ginger in front of me, when the bomb went off."

"Dear God. And then what happened?"

"I don't remember much. Apparently, Ginger was thrown back into me by the blast, and it was her weight that hurt my ribs. She came out of it with just some bruises, but I went down hard and was knocked out for a while. I never saw what happened to Alika. When I came fully conscious in the hospital and asked the doctor about him, he told me Alika 'wasn't as lucky' as I was, and I took that to mean he'd died." Sophie gulped, feeling nauseous. "His poor body, all it's been through because of me…"

"It is terrible what happened, but he is lucky to be alive if he was actually holding the device! And how was he when you saw him last?"

"I haven't seen him again." Sophie covered her face with her hands, hiding her shame.

"Oh, Sophie. My dear. This is why you are so haunted by this event." Dr. Wilson set aside her tablet and leaned forward. "The attempt on your life was horribly traumatic—you were injured and betrayed in a place where you thought you were safe, by an assassin using a name you thought you could trust…and you haven't been back to see Alika. To get closure with him."

"I can't." Sophie balled her hand into fists. "I just can't bear it. After what happened to him before." Sophie reminded Dr. Wilson of the time Alika was attacked by Assan Ang's henchmen. "This time, he lost an arm. I just can't deal with seeing him. I can't. I feel sick when I think of it." She held a hand over her stomach. "My father and I had a fight over it, and we never fight! He called me a coward. And he was right." Misery choked her, and Sophie hung her head.

"Sophie, the reason this is making you sick is that you know that your behavior is not…mature. You owe Alika your support, your concern, at least. He must be struggling emotionally. Losing a limb is huge."

"Every time I think of seeing him I...freak out, as Marcella would say. But our paths may be crossing anyway, at least indirectly. Esther Ka`awai, his grandmother, is connected with a new case Jake and I are working. I dread any interaction with her, even if she never knows I was the woman in the lobby with Alika when the bomb exploded."

"I'm not saying you have to see him in person. But you do have to reach out in some way. A phone call? What about a letter?"

"A letter." Relief at this idea almost made Sophie dizzy. "You're brilliant, Dr. Wilson! That I can do. And I will." For the first time, Sophie noticed the small wooden bowl of hand-molded clay figurines resting on the coffee table in front of her, along with a tray of golden beach sand. "What's this?"

"A projective tool some clients enjoy called 'sand tray therapy.' Very intuitive. You simply choose figures that appeal and set up a small scene. Sometimes insight comes to you in doing so."

All the figures were handmade, simple bisque shapes without features, glazed in clear. Sophie picked up the tallest feminine form in the bowl. She set the woman into the sand. She chose three male figures and set them around the woman in a triangle shape.

Bile rushed up her throat suddenly, and Sophie stood up. "Where's the bathroom again?"

Dr. Wilson pointed mutely to a small side door. Sophie ran in and slammed the door, bending over to retch into the pristine bowl.

When she was empty and had rinsed her mouth repeatedly, she glared at her wan reflection in the mirror over the sink. *"You're a terrible person,"* whispered that interior voice. *"A selfish coward. You should feel sick."*

A tap at the door. "Sophie, are you okay?"

"I'll be right out." Sophie turned on the fan. She splashed water on her face and used damp hands to scrunch her disordered curls back into shape. She'd dressed in a fresh Security Solutions "uniform" and needed to go into the office after this, but her knees felt wobbly and she was lightheaded. She opened the door to look at Dr. Wilson. "This trauma stuff is unpleasant."

She and Dr. Wilson resumed their places. Dr. Wilson cleared her throat. "Is there any chance you could be pregnant?"

Sophie leaned back abruptly to get the support of the couch in remaining upright. "No. I mean..." She and Jake had been using condoms, but there was always a chance something had gone wrong. And that time with Alika? *They hadn't used anything!* But it was just one time almost two months ago... Sophie covered her mouth with a hand, her eyes going wide. "No, surely not."

"Well, I was reviewing your physical symptoms while you were in the bathroom, and while they're consistent with PTSD, they're also consistent with pregnancy. When was your last period?"

"I don't know." Sophie's mind had gone completely blank. White noise filled her ears.

Dr. Wilson's gaze was level. "I can't recommend any medications for your depression until you rule out pregnancy. You're a young, healthy woman in her prime who's sexually active. This is something you need to tackle head-on. Take a test immediately. And if you're not pregnant, get on some birth control right away."

"I'm just upset. Traumatized. From everything." Sophie's lips felt numb. "I can't be pregnant. No."

"You have all the working parts. Just because you've got issues with your mother and you've never thought of yourself in this category doesn't mean it doesn't apply to you," Dr. Wilson said crisply.

"There's more to it than that." Sophie looked down at her clenched hands. "But I can't believe I was so stupid."

"Not stupid. Distracted," Dr. Wilson said. "You must have thought about children."

"I love children. But I never wanted to have them myself. Because Assan tried to get me pregnant. Over and over." Sophie felt sick again. She closed her eyes, breathing through it. *Another bit of nightmare from her past she hadn't let herself remember.* "Assan wouldn't let me use birth control. I would sneak and buy contraceptives when I could get out from the apartment, but eventually gave that up when he caught me and beat me for it. Five years of being raped and used, and I never conceived." She shook her head. "I just eventually assumed I couldn't get pregnant. It should have occurred to me that *he* was the problem."

"And thank God you didn't, or think how hard it would have been to escape," Dr. Wilson said. "Children are one of the many reasons women stay with an abuser. They're used as bargaining chips to get the woman to comply and keep her in the relationship."

Sophie nodded. "I burned incense in front of Quan Yin at our apartment, telling Assan I was praying to get pregnant...when the opposite was true. Even though he'd beat me when I got my period, I never stopped praying. And then one day I just felt my womb had closed. It would not betray me and open to him." She looked down to see her hands folded over her abdomen. "And then I just...forgot about it. Strange, I know."

"Dear girl. The mind does many strange things when trying to survive a terrible situation." Dr. Wilson glanced at the clock. "We are out of time. I hate to say goodbye with this kind of revelation, but you'd best go to the pharmacy right after this and get a test. Text me when you have the results."

The women hugged, and Sophie made an appointment for the following week with a request to get in sooner if there were any cancellations.

Out on the walkway at Dr. Wilson's little cottage office behind the University of Hawaii campus, standing beside torch ginger plantings in the overcast light of a Hilo day threatening rain, Sophie had to grab onto a nearby railing to stay upright as emotional overwhelm crashed in on her.

She might be pregnant.

CHAPTER NINE

THE SMELL of bleach barely covered an unpleasant ripeness of old blood floating on the air of the cavernous, historic Chang warehouse in downtown Hilo. Terence Chang observed the scene he had set as he waited for the heads of the different Chang business departments to arrive for the gathering he'd called.

He'd laid down a huge square of heavy plastic on the concrete floor. He'd moved a long koa wood table, used for generations of Chang gatherings, out of the conference room to this central spot. A white, waterproof tablecloth covered the expanse of wood and plastic folding chairs surrounded it. A floodlight beamed down on the table from above, casting the rest of the echoing space into shadow. A single water carafe was placed in the center of the table, and each seat was provided with a plastic glass, pen, and a copy of the agenda.

Terence had dressed for the occasion in a fitted charcoal gray suit with a narrow pinstripe and a red power tie. Wearing this level of formalwear, in Hawaii, sent a message. He walked to take his seat at the head of the table, and pressed his hands flat on the agenda and computer tablet to hide any tremble from his pounding pulse.

Terence's cousin Emma, his closest friend in the family business, stood in the doorway of the warehouse. Twenty-six-year-old Emma

47

had a maturity and composure beyond her years. She too, was dressed formally, wearing a floor-length muumuu in deep purple, the neckline trimmed in velvet. Multiple strands of pearls and *kahelelani* shells garlanded her slender throat. She met the different department heads at the door in a cheerful, firm manner, wanding them for weapons, collecting their firearms and phones, and directing them to the conference area.

"Looking so fly, cuz." Ikaika, a cousin in charge of one of the meth factories and Akane's surviving brother, approached Terence and took a seat next to him.

"Very Chicago gangster," Elektra, in charge of meth distribution, elaborated. "You always like to dress the part, Terence. I take it this means you're making a move on Byron's chair?"

Terence inclined his head, unsmiling, his only answer as the various department heads arrived, each of them assessing the space and members present. Chatter was overloud, a reverberation of nervousness echoing in the vast space.

When all the chairs were filled, Emma exited and shut the door. Terence hoped he was the only one who heard the clunk of a heavy lock on the outside.

Terence waited until everyone was seated, not responding to the occasional greetings, sallies and nervous jokes coming his way.

He waited with every appearance of patience, even as his hands sweated on his copy of the agenda.

He waited until the murmurs, comments, and casual trash talk finally ground to a halt and all eyes turned to him.

"You have all been provided a copy of today's agenda and a pen and space to make any notes needed." He gave the group a moment to look down at the agenda, printed with a bold new company name and logo: *Terence Chang and Associates*. The pen each had been provided was a commemorative Mont Blanc inscribed with the same company name in gold. "I direct your attention to item one on the agenda: new vision statement."

"This is bullshit!" His uncle Freddie Chang objected. Terence wasn't surprised that Akane's father was the first to challenge him, and he'd come prepared for opposition. He lifted a silenced Smith & Wesson 9mm from his lap, and shot his uncle between the eyes.

The loud pop of the pistol and the crash of his uncle's chair falling backward as the man hit the floor were the only sounds for a long moment—and then chaos erupted. Twenty cousins, uncles, aunts, and managers yelled, screamed, and jumped to their feet, scrambling for nonexistent phones and weapons.

Terence remained in his seat, the Smith & Wesson's butt resting on the tabletop because his hand was shaking so hard. His heart pounded in his ears. Adrenaline gave him hyper-focused vision that caught the slight, furtive movement of his cousin Ikaika's hand, as Akane's brother reached for a concealed weapon at his ankle.

The Smith & Wesson popped again, and Ikaika fell. Blood from the man's head splattered across Terence's aunt Mei. His aunt screamed loud and long, collapsing to her knees beside her fallen son, clutching his shoulders as she knelt beside her dead husband.

None of Akane's family was ever going to support him.

So he shot Mei and his cousin Elektra, too.

The table was short four members when the horrified group, after discovering that they were locked inside the building, returned to face Terence. "What the fuck, cuz?" one brave soul finally yelled.

Terence picked up his copy of the agenda and gestured with the pistol. "Shall we continue? Or would anyone else like to join them?"

The remaining members reluctantly resumed their seats amid the carnage. He waited until everyone had turned their attention back to him. "I believe we were going to review the new vision statement before that unfortunate, and entirely avoidable, interruption. But I'd just as soon clear the deadwood now than have to hunt people down later—so speak up if you have a problem with my leadership."

Terence gazed around the table, looking for any signs of disagreement. His determination felt like armor; he was completely committed to this course of action and he meant every word. If he needed to swim through blood to get to the door, then that's what needed to happen.

No one would meet his eyes. All were dutifully looking at their agendas. *Good.*

"The Chang operation is going to be cutting some aspects of the business, beginning with cessation of meth production." He waited for the murmurs to die down and continued. "Read this vision statement with me: 'Terence Chang and Associates exists to build and enrich the lives of its founding family, the Island of Hawaii, and our state, and to create healthy income streams to enrich our interests in perpetuity.'" He looked out at the silent, shocked faces surrounding him. "I am taking this company in a direction that's going to benefit not only us, but our island and community." He tapped his paper. "Note the word 'healthy.' Meth is unhealthy, and though it's easy money, it puts us at odds with those around us. All in favor of adopting the new vision statement, say 'aye.'" Terence's hand drifted down to rest on the pistol as his eyes flicked around the table. A chorus of reluctant "ayes" echoed around the room. *No accident that the Changs he'd eliminated were those running the meth operation.*

Terence wrinkled his nose against the increasingly sharp, coppery tang of blood in the air as the cooling bodies bled out. Sticky puddles formed around divots created by the chair legs on the plastic around their feet.

Looking at the mess had been a mistake.

He breathed through nausea and continued. "Let's move on to new business. We will be switching to legal marijuana growing, packaging, and distribution, using our former meth lab facilities and locations. Those not able to adapt their skills to the change in product are welcome to tender their resignations now." His hand had not left the pistol. No one got up or spoke. "I have arranged for a buyout of our current meth inventory and production equipment by Da Boyz on Oahu."

A groan met this. Da Boyz had been competition and a thorn in the Changs' side since the eighties, when the gang had moved into the Islands and developed a stranglehold on the construction trade and shipping on Oahu.

Terence ignored the muffled rumble of protest. "Da Boyz have agreed to give us more than fair market value for our product, and a bonus when the distribution and sale is completed. All of you here will be receiving a bonus from that sale. Across the board. Straight into each of your pockets. They are also giving us an ongoing cut for allowing them exclusive license to make meth in Hawaii, and an agreement not to compete with our *pakalolo* production."

For the first time, some animation and excitement began to show in the pale faces left around the table. "Just how much is this bonus going to be?" someone piped up.

"Counting heads here at the table? Probably a couple hundred grand apiece. And that is in addition to your usual percentages, which might have to be temporarily adjusted as we switch gears." He set down the agenda and steepled his fingers, making eye contact with each remaining person. "This has been a bit of a rough transition after Byron, but I assure you that, once we make the move, profits will be plentiful and the presence of cops minimal. Give me six months to turn this company around and head it in the direction of our new mission statement, and I promise you both prosperity and legitimacy in the business marketplace of the Big Island. No more looking over your shoulder for the next police raid."

"What about the gambling? The bingo, cockfighting, and mahjong?" Terence's intrepid aunt Suki asked. She was in charge of those illegal home gambling businesses that paid a cut to the Changs.

He smiled. "Okay, we'll still need to keep looking over our shoulders for some things. We're keeping the homegrown gambling."

"And the hookers?" Suki tipped her head. Her shiny dark eyes and demeanor reminded Terence of a mynah bird.

"We'll be phasing out those operations and replacing them with different businesses. I have some ideas. But not right away, and not today." Terence stood. "I think you all have enough change to deal with right now. Meeting dismissed."

The remaining members stood up. A few gasps and sobs were voiced as family members moved carefully around the bodies.

He kept his hand on the pistol, and his voice rang out after their retreating backs. "I've heard that Akane has escaped. If you hear from that psycho…tell Akane his family is waiting for him in hell, and I'll send him and anyone who helps him there too." Terence's flat tone carried weight. But he wasn't finished yet. "And in case you didn't know…I'm very good with technology and computers. All of you are being monitored. Consequences will be swift and lethal if you cross me. By the same token, rewards will be equally great."

The group shuffled silently toward the door. Emma unlocked it and opened it from the outside. A square of light seemed to appear at the end of a long dark tunnel.

Their weapons were not returned.

CHAPTER TEN

Sophie felt the pregnancy test weighing down her backpack as she walked into the Security Solutions office after her session with Dr. Wilson. The little white cardboard box she'd bought at the pharmacy almost seemed to be glowing, radioactive, advertising its presence through the nylon and her terrified conscience like a pulsing beacon.

Ridiculous. More of the depression talking, with its evil twin, anxiety. She didn't have to listen to the lies; the real situation was challenging enough.

She'd taken the time to freshen up and brush her teeth and change her shirt at the motel after the session, and she'd needed every minute to pull herself together.

Sophie stowed the backpack on a door hook and walked around to her desk to check the schedule, neatly printed out from their shared online calendar by the ever-efficient Felicia.

Out in the reception area, she could hear Jake and Felicia's voices rising and falling in that bantering, flirtatious cadence she was unable to participate in with any smoothness at all.

As she had remembered, a follow-up videoconference with their client Kim Kauwa was on the agenda. The woman was too busy to come in and meet with them, but Sophie needed to update her on some leads she had uncovered online regarding the money trail, and Jake's impressions after visiting the physical location of the Festival.

Jake entered, carrying a couple of old-fashioned root beers in glass bottles, their long necks beaded with moisture. "Brought you a little something."

Sophie had never seen anything look so delicious in her life. "Thanks, Jake."

She snatched one of the opened bottles out of his hand, tipped back her head, and guzzled.

"Well, now I know what to bring you when you're thirsty." Jake sounded amused.

Sophie set the half-empty bottle down on her desk and burped from the carbonation, covering her mouth with a hand. "Therapy is thirsty work."

Jake sat down in one of the two chairs fronting her desk, leaning it back on two legs as he sipped his root beer. "How did it go?"

"Like I said, therapy is work. Not fun." She wasn't about to fill him in any further.

"Last night was fun." He met her eyes meaningfully, a grin lurking.

Her cheeks went hot, remembering last night's passion. Clearly, he remembered it, too.

Jake would be angry and hurt if he found out that she and Alika had slept together, but the incident had happened before they were exclusive. She didn't need to feel guilty! *And hopefully she wasn't pregnant and would never have to tell him.*

The computer on Sophie's desk contained a voice audio communication feature in lieu of an antiquated intercom, and Sophie depressed a button on her keyboard to speak to Felicia. "Hey, Felicia. Can you initiate a call with our client, Kim Kauwa? And bill any time incurred to the Hawaii Tourism Authority account, please."

"Sure, boss." Felicia's voice sounded perky and agreeable, as she always did. Sophie wished she had even a fraction of the girl's positivity.

Felicia seemed like a great fit for Jake. She was smart, energetic, pretty, and probably didn't want a lot more out of life than a career, a white picket fence, and a couple of children…

Children. Augh! Sophie finished the root beer in a few giant swigs with her eyes on the computer's screen.

Jake scooted his chair up to her desk and leaned his upper body into her work area. His low, concerned voice cut across her negative reverie. "What's up? We had such a special time last night. What happened between when you left this morning, and now?"

Sophie shook her head mutely—there was too much to that subject to get into right now. She used her mouse to open up a new window in the client's file, and the incoming conference call icon pulsed. Sophie picked up a pair of cordless headphones and put them on, handing another pair to Jake, and hit the Accept Call feature. She turned the monitor to take in Jake as well as Kim's face appeared.

They greeted each other and exchanged social pleasantries.

"How's it going so far?" Kim's forehead exhibited a wrinkle between well-kept brows.

"I have been able to uncover a lead regarding the money trail online that I want to tell you about," Sophie said. "But I also want us both to hear from Jake regarding his impressions from the site visit."

"Yes, that was interesting," Jake said. "I enjoyed touring the venue for the event. I can tell it's well-attended, and the entire team putting it on seems very attentive and committed. The building and maintenance guy said security is pretty good with off-duty police officers, and only a few bathroom security concerns. I would like to know your impressions about the program manager, Ilima Cruz. She seems to be in a position to shunt funding wherever she wants it to go."

"Yes, she is in that position. But I would swear that Ilima is completely honest and dedicated to the vision of the Merrie Monarch as a vehicle for the promotion and preservation of Hawaiian culture. She would never do anything to endanger the Festival; in fact, rumor has it that she lost her marriage over it because she was so dedicated and overzealous." Kim looked like she might be a little overzealous herself. Dark circles under her eyes were visible even in the grainy video feed. Kim leaned forward, rubbing her temples with her fingertips. "What did you think of the old guy? The site manager?"

"Ando Bautista. He's quite a character. He seems to think there's something fishy with the financials, too. He said he remembers a lot more money being spent on visible promotion of the event than there has been this year. All of this, so far, is pointing to the leak being something related to marketing and advertising," Jake said.

"That's just what I was going to confirm to you, Kim." Sophie held up copies of bank statements that she had pulled from the Festival's accounts where the computer's camera could capture them for Kim to see. "The budget being given to the governing board is being followed—but the actual work and advertising being paid for is not being provided, even though it is on paper. Just don't ask any questions about how I got this information."

Kim shook her head. "I won't. What's next?"

"I think Jake and I should visit the advertising agency that's our main suspect. Go in undercover. Pitch ourselves as possible clients and see what we can see."

"That sounds good. Keep me posted!" They ended the call. Sophie busied herself taking some notes, waiting for Jake to get back to whatever he'd been doing.

Instead, he reached out for Sophie's hand. "Tell me what's wrong."

"Nothing." She tried to pull her hand away.

Jake wouldn't let go. "Look at me." He lifted her hand to his lips and nibbled on her fingertip. Sensation shot through Sophie and lit her up. *Those gray eyes were hypnotizing her.* Damn those lashes of his, they were like black winter branches around an icy pond...

"Not in the office," she breathed.

Jake held Sophie's gaze, kissing a path across her palm and onto her wrist with his warm, supple lips. "Mm. We never did break in this desk," he murmured.

The door opened silently, and Felicia stood there, holding a file. Her face drained of color as she took in the scene, meeting Sophie's eyes. The receptionist withdrew abruptly, shutting the door.

Sophie tried to tug her hand away again. "Felicia saw you doing that."

"So what?" Jake was intent on her, oblivious to the heart he'd just broken. "I have a couple of apartments I want us to go see. It's time for us to get out of that motel."

"We're not moving in together, Jake."

"Why not?"

Sophie swallowed, feeling sick again. "Because. It's too soon."

"Explain to me how it makes sense for us to go through the expense and hassle of renting two places when you know we'll just end up spending the night at one place or the other."

Sophie shut her eyes as he resumed making love to her hand like he had all the time in the world. Delicious ripples of feeling moved up her arm and over her body, and headed south from there.

So much work to find her own place, deal with all the paperwork and applications, expense, and hassle. But living together? So much more of a commitment than dating exclusively. *On the other hand, they might be having a child together...*

She yanked her hand away and tucked it into her lap, where it tingled as if separate from the rest of her body. "I agree we need to get out of the motel, but I don't feel ready to move in with you."

"Fine. I kind of guessed you might get stubborn about it." Jake didn't even sound annoyed—he just settled back in his chair with an air of getting down to business. He took out his phone. "I found two apartments in the same building. Ocean views on Hilo Bay, close to running trails, and pet friendly for the dogs. Now that we've finished the meeting with Kim, we can go look at the units. I already made an appointment."

Gratitude that he was not only accepting her boundary but helping with the challenges of moving filled her. Sophie leaned across the desk to kiss him. "Can we get some lunch, too? I'm really hungry all of a sudden."

CHAPTER ELEVEN

AKANE CHANG THREW BACK his head and howled his grief. *"Nooo!"*

He turned and hit the heavy workout bag, dangling beside him, with a flurry of blows. The padded gloves he wore thumped like bullets hitting flesh.

He had no family left: his parents, his brother, his closest cousin —all dead.

He had never expected Terence to make this kind of balls-out deadly move in a million years. Killing his own relatives in cold blood in front of a roomful of witnesses? It was the act of a much harder man than Akane had ever imagined his cousin to be. And now Terence had the whole board eating out of his bloody hand with a combination of fear and reward.

He hit and kicked and thrashed on the bag until his first paroxysm of emotion was expended.

Lee Chow, deliverer of the bad news, cleared his throat awkwardly. "I'm sorry, man."

"You're sorry?" The unreasoning beast of rage roared up through Akane's veins and gave him super strength. He leapt upon his associate, raining blows on Chow's body until the man's defensive posture, with his arms up over his face, finally reminded Akane that this was no enemy.

He heaved himself away from Chow and stalked around the small, empty gym, swearing vengeance, muttering the names of his lost family members in a litany that gave him little solace.

He wished he could kill Terence's parents, but his aunt and uncle were already gone, collateral damage in a business dispute years ago. Instead, he would have the blood of anyone Terence had ever known or loved. He'd go after Terence's favorite family connections. He knew where they lived. He'd draw out their pain and enjoy every minute of their suffering. Akane's gloved hands opened and shut in anticipation.

He'd leave Terence for last, so his cousin could rage and grieve as Akane was doing now.

Akane reached Lee Chow, groaning on the floor. He leaned over and patted Chow's shoulder awkwardly. "Sorry, man. Didn't mean to go off on you like that. I've got a major bonus for you, but I need some information first."

CHAPTER TWELVE

THE BUILDING MANAGER'S keys rattled as he opened the door of the first unit for Jake and Sophie. He reeked of cigarettes and the greasy chicken they'd interrupted him eating when they arrived for the showing, and Jake noticed Sophie's nose scrunched in obvious distaste as they stood downwind. "It's a studio. Best feature is the view," the man said.

A simple room with linoleum flooring, a kitchenette, and a bathroom, the place did have a deck with a sliding glass door that looked out over Hilo Bay. The soft gauze of "vog" cast a powdered gold glow lit by afternoon sunlight falling over the gently swaying palms, Hilo Bay's gleaming water in the distance. The busy thoroughfare of their office was only blocks away; it was a convenient location, even if not the most beautiful building. Sophie looked around at the simple space. "I think I'd like a little more room than this."

"We were going to look at the one bedroom, too," Jake told the manager.

"Sure." The man glanced at their joined hands. "You could save money by sharing. As roommates. Or just shacking up."

Jake suppressed a grin—*the guy was making his case for him.*

Sophie was testy. "Your opinion is not relevant, sir. Please just show us the unit."

The man shrugged and led the way out of the studio down an open exterior corridor to the next unit. This one had a separate bedroom, living room, and a galley-style kitchen. Sophie's gaze darted around the space. "I'll take this one, Jake, if you don't mind."

He knew how she would furnish it: with blackout curtains in the bedroom, triple locks on the door, and not a lot of furniture—if any. *He'd shop for both of them.*

"I like the studio better, so this works out perfectly." Jake squeezed Sophie's hand, suppressing the twinge of hurt he still felt over her insistence on separate spaces. She'd tried to tug her hand away during the appointment several times, but he found that if he just persisted gently, she usually warmed up. Her standoffishness was a habit as much as anything, and he relished every time she let him get closer.

But today, something was definitely up with her.

They'd had amazing lovemaking after the talk at the restaurant, but Sophie'd come to work from that therapy session at Dr. Wilson's looking pale, shaky, and totally shut down. He'd tried to get her to open up, but no go.

He'd give her space, but not for long.

Secrets were toxic. They eroded trust, and trust was the foundation for everything that mattered. He'd set out to prove to Sophie that he could be trusted, and so far, so good. That she'd shared the situation with her mother and the project she and Hamilton were working on was huge—but he wanted to know her emotional secrets, too, even if they hurt.

Even if they involved her feelings for Alika.

They wrapped up the appointment by completing applications for the two units, then heading back down to the white Security Solutions SUV.

"Think we should let the dogs out before we go to the ad

agency?" Jake asked, getting behind the wheel. "We're passing right by the motel."

"Good idea. Can you do it? I'm so tired; I just need a small nap." Sophie reclined her seat. "Ten minutes. That's all I need."

"No problem."

Sophie reached into that backpack she carried everywhere and took out a black sleep mask. She slid it on, reclined her seat, and by the time he'd pulled the SUV out of the parking lot, she was asleep, her long body curled sideways on the seat facing him.

Nope, they hadn't slept much last night, and all of that activity had wiped her out. Jake smiled at the memory.

He navigated back to the motel and rolled down the vehicle's windows, parking in the shade of the motel's trademark banyan tree so Sophie would stay cool while she rested. He put Ginger and Tank on their leashes and took them for a short run, letting the ad agency they were investigating know they were going to be a little late.

The dogs cavorted and tugged, pausing to pee on every tree and patch of grass. They'd been able to let the animals stay together since they'd rented adjoining rooms, but once they were in their separate apartments, they'd likely have to be split up. He didn't think the dogs would like that.

Jake put the dogs back in the room and gently shook Sophie. "Hey, Soph. Hate to wake you, but we have to get into our disguises as a couple shopping for an advertising firm."

"Oh." Sophie knuckled her eyes. She was so beautiful, even rumpled and sleepy—okay, *especially* rumpled and sleepy. He loved her that way—it brought out all his caveman instincts. Carrying her back to the room seemed like a fun option, if she'd let him.

Jake opened her car door, hoping to grab her up, but Sophie got out and stood, stretching her arms and yawning widely. "Thanks for letting me nap."

She picked up her pack and headed for the motel room as he closed the vehicle's windows. He pulled the magnetic Security Solutions signs off the doors so they could go incognito as clients to Coconut Wireless Advertising & Marketing.

Back in the motel room, Jake changed into a button-down aloha shirt in a subdued tropical print and chino shorts as the water ran in the bathroom and Sophie showered. He glanced at the backpack, sitting innocuously on her bed. *What was in there that she guarded so closely?*

Was he really considering having a peek inside?

Yep, he was. He'd always been too curious; even his mama said so. Made him a good investigator.

Jake unzipped the top of the pack and peeked in.

Nothing more than he'd expected—a solid-state storage drive, a couple of stick drives. Her wireless headphones. A rolled jump rope for those exercise breaks she liked to take. A small flashlight, a pocketknife. Some electrical tape and a blue coil of internet cable. A couple of wallets that she used for her identities. A bag of dog treats. Jake moved the bag of treats aside with a finger and froze at the sight of the small white box concealed beneath it.

A pregnancy test?

Jake's heart rate jacked like he'd spotted a rattlesnake. He recoiled, sweat breaking out over his body. He zipped the pack shut and adjusted it to make sure it looked untouched, feeling horrible that he'd violated her privacy...*and yet.*

A pregnancy test? That sure as shit affected him too!

What the hell should he do?

"Holy Mary," he muttered, returning momentarily to his family's Catholic roots. He collapsed on the end of his bed, dropping his head into his hands. Tank got up and came to lick Jake's arms, sensing his agitation. Jake pushed the dog away even as he felt happiness burst forth from somewhere deep inside, bubble up through his body, and out through his face in a huge grin.

Sophie might be pregnant, and he might be a daddy.

He'd always wanted to be a daddy.

But he had to tamp his excitement down. Hide his thoughts.

Conceal that he had a clue. Because Sophie would not take kindly to his snooping, that was for sure.

Sophie came out of the bathroom wrapped in a towel. Her color was better, her eyes brighter. "I guess I needed that nap." She eyeballed him. "You look like a tourist."

Jake held out a huarache-clad foot. "Too much?"

"I never see anyone but visitors wear those. Aren't we supposed to be residents?" Sophie dropped the towel to the floor in front of the room's tacky bureau and rummaged in a drawer.

Jake enjoyed the sight of Sophie naked: bending over to open a lower drawer, taking out underwear and stepping into them, tugging them up over her slim thighs to hug her perfect butt. *What this woman did to him...* She slid her arms into a plain black bra, clipping it in front.

He assessed her breasts as she turned in his direction. *They seemed bigger.* But maybe he was imagining things, with this new knowledge. She was definitely filling out again after that bad time she'd been through out alone on the lava, getting back to a healthy weight...his mind raced, counting the weeks since they'd first slept together on their previous job.

If she was pregnant, it had to have happened then. Officially becoming a couple was too soon...but what the hell did he know? He'd have to Google the whole damn thing.

Jake's mind was a kaleidoscope of whirling thoughts that he hid with difficulty as Sophie finished primping and turned to face him in her Mary Watson disguise: a floral sundress and sandals, big Jackie O sunglasses, and a straw hat. She picked up her backpack. "Please stop staring at me, Jake."

"Nope. I like staring at you." Jake swallowed his grin with difficulty as she elbowed him walking past. He followed her out the door, wondering how the hell he'd get through the days until she decided to tell him what was going on with that little white box.

CHAPTER THIRTEEN

SOPHIE WALKED up the weathered wooden steps of the Coconut Wireless Advertising & Marketing office, located on the Hamakua side of Hilo in a restored plantation cottage. Prepared to be suspicious, Sophie was charmed instead, as she gazed around the tidy, square building with its plethora of sheltering tree ferns, weathered tikis and Buddhas, and pots of blooming orchids.

Jake, a wall of heat at her elbow, verbalized Sophie's thoughts. "Sweet place."

The front office was the former living room. A pretty young receptionist waved them in and offered them tea and coffee. They declined and were soon shown into a back office.

A woman with a face and figure like one of the grinning Buddhas on the building's porch greeted them. "Welcome to Coconut Wireless! I'm Penny Chang. How can we help you?"

Sophie felt a *ping!* of anxiety go off as she shook the woman's soft, plump hand. *Penny Chang had to be related to the crime family.* "I'm Mary. Mary Watson. And this is my boyfriend, Lance O'Connell."

"Hey there," Jake said, with a Southern drawl that sounded entirely real. "Love your place."

"Oh yes. This house was our family home when I was growing up, and it needed remodeling. I decided it was perfect for an office, instead." Penny bustled around to sit down at her desk, a large koa table with a computer on one end. "What can I help you with today?"

Sophie glanced at Jake, who picked up the thread of their planned spiel. "We are planning a major event to alert corporate and other customers to our new business. We're a travel agency located in Hilo. We specialize in putting together one-of-a-kind travel packages for groups and businesses."

Penny slipped on a pair of reading glasses and pulled out a yellow pad from a small stacking organizer. She grinned up at them, looking more Buddha-like than ever. "Oh, I have a perfect plan in mind. We can do print and online exposure for you and your event, and also some signage around town and the dock area where travelers and visitors would see it." She slipped off the glasses to make eye contact with Sophie. "How did you hear about us?"

"We are big fans of the Merrie Monarch Festival." Sophie smiled back at the woman—it was impossible not to. "We heard you handle their PR. Did you do that big billboard over by the airport? Very attractive."

"Well, it's not a billboard," Penny temporized. "Billboards are against the law in Hawaii. But it is the maximum signage size allowed."

"I loved the image of the hula dancers," Jake enthused. "We thought we'd like to get a package similar to what you provided for the Festival. You must really blanket the state and beyond to draw the kind of crowds into Hilo that the Festival brings!"

"The Festival is a unique event." Penny was still smiling, but it had gone stiff at the edges of her mouth. "Merrie Monarch has a life of its own, a following that is dedicated to supporting it. Not much is needed to keep it visible in the public's eye and imagination."

"You don't have a big budget with them?" Sophie raised her brows inquiringly. "I know I saw that sign by the airport. What else do you provide for them?"

"Well." Penny put her glasses on and looked down at her notes. "As I was saying, these two things are apples and oranges. One is a big, annual, well-established event and has a lot of momentum and huge local support. Your event? Forgive me for being blunt, but no one cares about it. It's going to need a lot of money and effort to get you even a margin of the same kind of visibility. I'm thinking TV and radio spots. Ads in the newspaper and local publications. An online presence on all the popular Hilo and Hawaii travel sites. You're talking fifty to a hundred grand, depending on what options you choose."

"Hmm." Jake glanced at Sophie. "We've got some venture capital funds, but I think we should get a budget from you, a rough outline of what you could do for what kind of spend, before we make a final decision. Right, honey?"

Sophie liked the sound of the endearment—it definitely gave her a warm feeling to play the part and call Jake her boyfriend in public. "That seems like a reasonable plan. But first, tell us about your staffing. Do you have many people working for you, to put all this in motion?" She gestured to the closed door. "I didn't see anyone but your receptionist."

"We have several other employees, but most of them operate remotely. A lot of the work can be done via computer and phone," Penny said. "What are your deadlines? Branding? I need a lot of information on your company to come up with a proper package."

"Our date is flexible." Jake was already getting to his feet. He took Sophie's hand and drew her up to stand beside him. "We're just shopping right now. Please put together your best offers for different spend levels, send it to this email address, and we'll get back to you." He handed her a business card with a name and logo they'd created. *Follow Me Faraway Travel Agency* was printed on the card, along with a burner phone number and email they'd use for this investigation.

"By the way. Are you related, by any chance, to Terence Chang?" Sophie tilted her head demurely. "I met Terence in college, and he told me he was from Hilo. I thought we could look him up since we are new to the area."

Penny's smile was a mere twitch of the lips this time. "Terence is my cousin. But then, so is half the island."

Sophie chuckled politely. "Does he still live around here?"

"He does." Penny's dark brown eyes glinted coldly. "You want his number? Look in the phone book."

"There will be many, many Changs in the information database." Sophie frowned. "That is not helpful."

Jake cut in. "Ah, ha! Not your favorite person. We get that. Friends you choose, and family you're stuck with. I know the feeling. Thanks for your time, and we'll look for your estimate on email, or give us a jingle on the phone."

"You'll hear from me," Penny said. Sophie felt a shiver zip up her spine at the woman's glare. Jake tugged Sophie's hand, and she followed him out of the building and down to their SUV.

Evening cast long shadows over the narrow, two-lane, winding road as they headed back toward the Banyan Tree Motel with Jake in the driver's seat. "What was that about?" Jake asked. "You spooked her. What does Terence have to do with anything?"

"I don't know." Sophie rubbed the scar on her cheekbone, her gaze on the tall, swaying grasses and spreading albizia trees edging the highway as Jake drove. "I just think Terence might be useful to us here. I know he has been trying to go legit. I've been thinking of reaching out to him."

"But why would he help us with anything? You testified against his cousin!"

Sophie shook her head. "Perhaps it was a foolish mistake. But now we know that Penny Chang is not a friend of Terence. Maybe that could be useful."

"And maybe she's going to call him and tell him a couple of suspicious *haoles* were asking about him," Jake grumbled. "I doubt she even does the estimate for us."

"We'll have to feed her more info about our travel company.

Maybe even put down a deposit. But I could hear in her tone when talking about the Merrie Monarch what her rationale is for not spending all the funds. She thinks the Festival doesn't need the advertising. She doesn't think stealing that money is wrong."

"I heard that loud and clear, too," Jake said.

Sophie yawned. "I took that nap but I'm still tired. I wish we could finish the day now, but I need you to take me back to the office. I have to meet Hamilton for more work on our confidential project."

Jake tightened his mouth but said nothing.

Sophie reclined her seat and curled up, tucking her hands under her chin. *Was tiredness a sign of early pregnancy?*

She really needed to just find the courage to take that test.

They drove toward Hilo in silence, and Sophie fell asleep again.

CHAPTER FOURTEEN

CONNOR STOOD in the doorway of the company jet, watching Sophie approach across the tarmac. He had flown back to Hilo from Oahu after meeting with Security Solutions department heads and reviewing quarterly statements. He'd already done a run around the rim of Kilauea Volcano, just to get the kinks worked out from all that sitting, and now, he savored the sight of Sophie walking toward him in one of her Mary Watson dresses.

Sophie's legs had a beautiful line revealed by the dress. The sunset gleamed on her golden skin, the well-turned definition of her arms. She'd always reminded him of a human equivalent of his Doberman: sleek, graceful muscle, and elegant proportions.

Connor had spent weeks alone with Sophie on his private island as she recovered from her ordeal on the lava flow and awaited the Chang trial. His dog, Anubis, was good company at his private paradise, but far from enough—he'd missed Sophie acutely, and it had been hell trying to keep busy since he'd seen her last.

Trying to keep from watching her through various surveillance channels. *Trying not to imagine her in bed with Jake.*

There was a little more spring in Sophie's step than he remembered seeing since the bomb went off on Oahu. He hated to even imagine how close she'd come to dying that day.

Connor was trying to protect Sophie any way he could—but discovering that Akane Chang had escaped was a major complication.

Akane was wily, staying off the grid and out of sight. Other than a few facial recognition pings from Oahu street cameras and at the Honolulu Airport, Connor had not been able to find any trace of him.

Now they needed to move forward with Sophie's involvement with the Yām Khûmkạn, Thailand's shadowy, cultlike spy agency.

Sophie ascended the jet's steps and greeted him. "You could have come to meet with me at the office downtown, now that I've told Jake we're working on a special project."

"I prefer the increased privacy and security here on the plane." Connor's body tightened as Sophie slid by him into the interior of the plane's main area. She seated herself at the built-in dinette table and unfolded a small tablet produced from her backpack.

Connor picked up his own tablet and joined her.

"What's the plan?" Her eyes were down, her fingers flying as she launched an app.

"Our next step is to set up a meet with Pim Wat." He blew out a breath. "I've been trying to locate Akane Chang, but I can't get a solid lead on him."

"That son of a goiter-riddled goat!" Sophie glared up at him, clearly enraged at Akane's escape. "That maniac needs to die. Did you find out how he got loose?"

"Classic insider breakout. He's being hidden by Chang connections somewhere in Honolulu, I think. However, I've heard there's a shake-up happening in the Chang empire. Terence Chang is stepping up to lead the family, and he's no friend of Akane. I'm sitting tight for now and watching what happens. Maybe Pim Wat might be interested in doing something about him."

"What do you mean?" Sophie's golden-brown eyes narrowed.

"Are you suggesting that I manipulate my mother into killing someone for me?"

Connor tapped his chin with the finger. "A crude way of putting it, but yes. People like Pim Wat have their uses."

"Spoken like the Ghost." Sophie snorted. "I'll fight my own battles, thank you very much. I will contact her after our discussion, though. Should I wear a camera or recording device? What do you think the CIA is going to want from us?"

"From my talks with them, they will want to monitor all interactions. I don't know whether you will be searched by Pim Wat or her team, though. I wouldn't want you to take the risk of going in with a wire or other recording device until she trusts you. And you want her trust, need it really. We will set up the meet in a public area where I can video and record your conversation. I have a location picked out. I will transmit the intel to the CIA if they require it."

"I already know that Pim Wat wants me to go to Thailand to do the programming for the Yām Khûmkạn. It's a setup; I won't do it."

"Agreed. That woman cannot be trusted, even though she is your mother. Tell her that you have a secure location from which you can access and work on her computer systems. You don't need to go anywhere, and you shouldn't."

"And where would that secure location be, exactly?" Sophie cocked her head. "I don't have anywhere secure enough to deploy programs like DAVID currently, let alone a place to tinker with Thailand's government's black ops software."

"I've already sent workmen to the Security Solutions extension office to put in state-of-the-art rigs and load them with top-end encryption and multiple VPN routing capabilities. We're making that third office into a computer room, and we'll increase the security of the office location at the same time."

Sophie smiled. "That is most thoughtful of you, Connor. I can always count on you to anticipate what I need."

The compliment lit something inside of Connor, expanding his chest painfully. His heart rate sped up, but he concealed his reaction as he gave a brief nod. "Make the call to Pim Wat. I've got you covered with a location for the meet, and everything you need to stay safe. Set it for tomorrow morning."

CHAPTER FIFTEEN

Day Three

THE NEXT MORNING SOPHIE WALKED, holding Ginger's leash, into the pocket park near Hilo Bay that Connor had chosen for the meet with Pim Wat. She wore a Mary Watson dress and the swish of the skirt felt good against her legs. She sat on a bench and took out her tablet, holding it on her lap. Ginger relaxed beside her. Sophie enjoyed the chirp of cardinals, the coo of doves, and the chatter of a few mynah birds hopping on the grass. The dog's soft golden head rested against Sophie's leg as she scrolled, reviewing news items on social media, her eyes scanning the grounds from under the brim of a sun hat that wasn't yet needed in the day's early light.

Palm trees stood still as graceful guardians, surrounding an immaculate open grassy area. A small, chuckling fountain in the shape of a dolphin splashed into a pond filled with slow-moving koi. Tropical plantings enhanced the intimate little park—but the place's best feature was the motel directly across the street, where Connor surveilled her from a second story window.

An elderly woman leaning on a cane approached, wearing baggy, worn clothing, her hands hidden in net gloves. A ball cap shielded her face. Familiar with this incarnation of her mother's, Sophie ignored Pim Wat until her mother sat down. Ginger got up and approached, whining and thrusting her nose into Pim Wat's lap for a pet.

"Still keeping this mangy animal, I see," she hissed, thrusting Ginger's head away. "She makes you a target."

"A target for Akane Chang?" Sophie tugged Ginger away. "Surprised you care, Mother."

Pim Wat scowled, a crease of her forehead, a pucker of her full mouth. Her face appeared as young as Sophie's in the deep shade of the hat. "You have no idea what I've done, and will do, to keep you safe."

"How touching. Pardon my skepticism while I recall how you sold me in marriage to a sadistic psychopath to be tortured and used as a bargaining chip for your precious agency."

"We've been over this. Old news. Move on, Sophie Malee." Pim Wat's dark eyes gleamed in the hat's shade. Her hands gripped the head of the cane so hard the bone of her knuckles showed through the mesh of her gloves. "When can you come to Thailand and execute the computer contract we need you for?"

"I told you I'm not going anywhere near the Yām Khûmkạn compound. Security Solutions has set up a computer lab for me with all the firewalls, protocols, and data storage I need to complete your project." Sophie made sure her body was turned to face the window across the street, where Connor was observing and recording their meeting with a surveillance device. "Give me the name of someone in the organization who is handling your online presence. Someone that I can communicate with about what I'm setting up. Someone who knows your computers and what is needed to optimize and archive your data securely."

Pim Wat's pretty mouth tightened. "I could just...take you."

Sophie narrowed her eyes. "Really, Mother? You'd kidnap me to do your dirty job in a third world country, surrounded by assassins?

Because I've seen the Yām Khûmkạn stronghold, and short of taking me by force, I won't be going anywhere near it."

"How did you find that location?" Pim Wat's voice was sharp.

Sophie shrugged. "The world is a small place these days."

They exchanged a hostile stare.

Pim Wat sighed and looked away. "I had no idea that you'd grow up to be so difficult." She reached into some hidden pocket and removed a stick drive. "All the information you need to get started is here. Your first payment will be wired into the bank account of your choosing." She set the drive on the bench beside her and got up, walking away with an entirely authentic-looking hunched posture and nary a backward glance.

Sophie swiped the drive into her own pocket and got up, tweaking Ginger's leash. "Come, girl. We have work to do."

Striding across the park, conscious of Connor's electronic eyes on her, Sophie made an effort not to hunch her shoulders or betray the unease that her mother's threat had loosed.

She would have to get right to work on the project, whatever it was, and prove that she didn't need to be kidnapped and carried halfway around the world to do good work.

Sophie had not found the courage the night before to take the pregnancy test. Pleading tiredness, she'd said good night to Jake and slept in her own room, away from him, for the first time since they'd been together.

And though she'd wanted to be alone, she hadn't slept well; she tossed and turned, unable to stop thinking of how close she'd come to suicide, alone on that lava field. Worrying and wondering if she might be pregnant.

She'd had that emergency ketamine treatment for her depression —and if she was expecting, could it have caused developmental problems?

Then, the explosion at her father's building. The stress, the medications she'd needed for her injured ribs—all of those things could impact a developing fetus.

She had to find the courage to find out. She was torturing herself about something that might not even be a problem.

Ginger tugged at the leash, bringing Sophie back to earth as she headed to the Security Solutions SUV. She had to wrestle the dog into the vehicle's back hatch area. Once seated inside, she called Connor. "Well, did you get the meeting recorded all right?"

"Yes. Seemed to go well. She accepted your alternate work site." She could hear the rattle of a keyboard in the background—Connor was always multitasking. "Let me know what's on that stick drive once you open it up."

"I will." Sophie gathered her thoughts. "You don't have to hang around here in Hilo, Connor. I'm sure you have important things to do."

"This *is* important. I'll be here on the Big Island until Akane Chang is captured, and we have a good read on Pim Wat and her organization. I'm not going anywhere." Irritation colored his tone.

"But what about Anubis? You have a home—your island. Your mission. You can't keep living on that plane indefinitely…"

"Almost sounds like you care, Sophie," Connor said harshly, and ended the call.

Sophie winced, hearing an echo of her own words to her mother in his parting sentence.

CHAPTER SIXTEEN

TERENCE mentally braced himself as he picked up the ultra-private phone he used only for his informant network. Good news seldom came through this line. "This is T."

"T. I like that! Terence, I thought I should give you a call." His cousin Penny's receptionist had one of those breathy, little-girl voices he'd recognize anywhere. "Your cuz won't call you, but I thought you should know a couple of *haoles* were asking about you. Supposedly they have a travel agency business, but I smell cop. Penny did too."

"Tell me more." Terence grabbed a pen and jotted down the girl's descriptions of the visitors: a tall, pretty, mixed-race woman, and a large Caucasian man with "a military vibe." He jotted down *Follow Me Faraway Travel Agency* and the email and phone number they'd left on a business card.

"You asked me to listen in on Penny, so this is what I got. The two were asking her about the Merrie Monarch Festival and what she did for them. Then the woman, Mary Watson, pretended to be a classmate of yours and asked to meet up with you. Penny told me she thought they were undercover cops. She said she'd just let nature take its course, hoping they catch you doing something wrong. I get the feeling Penny hopes getting busted is the least of what happens to you. No offense."

"None taken. You did right, gorgeous." Terence injected his voice with a sexy enthusiasm he didn't feel. This girl was angling for a relationship as well as a tip to her paycheck, but he'd never cozy up to a woman willing to sell out her employer even if it benefited him. "Look for a little something special from me in the mail."

Ending the call, Terence tightened his lips. *The last thing he needed right now was a pair of cops sniffing around.*

His shoulders, arms, and back still ached from dealing with the corpses of his relatives. Other than Emma, there was no one he trusted enough to help him dispose of the bodies. The complete disappearance of an entire family would muddy the waters of whether or not murder had been committed, an important element with so many witnesses still running around.

Terence had done his internet research and found a way to get rid of the bodies permanently. *That didn't mean it hadn't been hard and grisly work.* He flexed sore hands, wishing he could cleanse his mind as well as he'd been able to wash his skin. But there was no erasing memory.

Thank God for Emma. She had nerves of steel and an iron stomach. His cousin was officially his right-hand woman.

Terence opened a browser window on one of the three monitors he had set up in the office that had been Byron's. He searched the name and contact info of the travel agency. A basic website popped up, but digging a little deeper uncovered that it had only been opened days ago. Who were these people, and what did they want with him? Be interesting to take the bull by the horns and find out.

Terence called the phone number that Penny's receptionist had given him.

A woman with a sexy accent answered, "Follow Me Faraway Travel Agency."

"This is Terence Chang. I heard you were asking about me?"

A short, charged pause. "Oh. Terence. What a surprise to hear from you, and how lovely. Your cousin must have let you know I was asking about you. This is Mary Watson. We were in school together. University of Washington, class of 2009."

Terence narrowed his eyes. "I don't remember you."

A husky chuckle. Her voice was oddly familiar. "I remember you. You're very good with computers."

"I should be. I majored in computer science." Terence relaxed back into his chair, flipping a pencil on his fingers. *Play along, see where it goes.* "My cousin seems to think you and your partner are cops. Glad to hear that isn't the case."

"Cops? Oh no." Mary Watson's laugh was strained. "I can't imagine why she thought that. We're possible clients. Just new to the area."

"Well. Maybe we should have a beer and catch up." The longer the woman spoke, the surer he was that he knew her... Tall, pretty, mixed-race, with a foreign accent? *Sophie Ang!*

The female investigator who'd testified against Akane was out fishing again.

He'd also tangled with the woman a few years ago when she was in the FBI—Ang was a talented hacker and sleuth. She'd infiltrated his online business and uncovered his role in a shady website. The whole thing had nearly derailed his attempt to go legit and sent him to jail.

Terence had also been in the back of a police car observing when Sophie and her military jock of a partner hauled Akane out of the jungle. Since then, he'd followed everything about Akane's case with obsessive interest, even watched Byron's button cam recordings of the trial, discovered on his deceased cousin's laptop.

"I'm sorry, but I can't take the time for a beer right now. Lance and I are moving this weekend. Lance's my partner, but also my boyfriend." Ang sounded flustered. *She knew he'd recognize her if he saw her.* "So much to do with our business launch, too. Can I call you again when things settle down?"

"Sure." Terence smiled as he recited his confidential phone's digits for her.

Sophie Ang was here in Hilo. And she was the perfect target to lure Akane out of the shadows, and possibly get him captured.

Terence ended the call and bent forward, his fingers flying as he searched for any Hilo connections to Sophie Ang. Moments later, the Security Solutions website came up with a new page added, listing a location in downtown Hilo and staffed by Sophie Ang and Jake Dunn. Each of their impressive work histories was summarized.

Terence dragged the info to a file he already had on Sophie, containing clips from the trial he'd culled from Byron's button cam coverage of that event.

Revenge for her testimony would be at the top of Akane's hit list. Terence had heard the venom his cousin had spouted as he was hauled out of the courtroom.

Julie Weathersby's name had also been one of those his maniac cousin shouted as he promised vengeance. Terence had already contacted Julie's parents to tell them that Akane had escaped. He'd suggested a long, foreign vacation for Julie—with bodyguards.

Terence was taking every precaution he could to protect anyone he cared about. He'd warned his ex-girlfriends, and Emma was stashed in his fortified house with his dogs and a team of mercenaries he'd hired from the Mainland.

Terence was in a war, and it was just beginning. Providing Akane with a target and flushing him out by pitting him against a couple of trained investigators with ties to the FBI was a smart strategy.

Still, he felt a twinge of regret as he texted the Security Solutions location info to a cousin whom he knew would pass it on to Akane. "Good luck, Sophie Ang," he whispered. "I hope you beat him."

CHAPTER SEVENTEEN

JAKE PERUSED the aisles of the local Target store, looking for items for his and Sophie's apartments and loading them onto a flatbed cart. It seemed ridiculous and redundant to buy two televisions, two futon foldout bed combos, two of everything, in fact—when hopefully, Sophie would soon be moving into his apartment.

Or, more likely, he would be moving into hers, since hers was bigger.

But Sophie'd begged off from sleeping with him last night, not a good sign. And this morning, he hadn't had so much of a glimpse of her before she took off again for the secret project she was working on with Sheldon Hamilton.

He was also trying not to obsess about the pregnancy test.

All of it was making his chest ache. Jake rubbed his left pec, kneading the knot of the bullet scar near his shoulder, trying to relieve a tightness he couldn't seem to shake.

Done with the shopping, he loaded the home furnishings into, and on top of, the Security Solutions SUV and headed back to the apartment building. He would unload the basics he'd bought, and they could spend some time that evening setting up the apartments. He was eager to be out of the motel with its lumpy beds and taint of mildew. *Maybe they'd even spend the night in the new place —together.*

Hamilton had given them a housing stipend as part of their salary packages, and Jake had cash deposits ready for the landlord, along with a little something to keep their addresses from being revealed to anyone who came asking. They had rented the apartments under their aliases as a precaution, and Jake planned to continue to pay the rents in cash.

He needed someone to talk to. Someone who had his best interests at heart. Someone loyal, and loving, who would give him no bullshit. There was only one person like that in his life: his sister Patty.

Jake speed dialed her number once he'd pulled up at the parking lot of the apartment building that would soon be their new address.

"Jake?" Patty's voice sounded surprised when she answered. "Everything OK?"

"Hey sis. I know I don't call often enough, but believe it or not, there's no emergency. I'm just needing some more sisterly relationship advice. What you told me last time was so good—it actually worked."

"Yay, that's great! I've been meaning to call you myself and find out what happened with that coworker you told me you had feelings for."

"We're together now. She asked me, and I quote, 'to be her lover.'" Jake couldn't help grinning.

"That's awesome…if that's what you want?" Patty sounded a little worried. "I know you said she was kind of hard to pin down."

"Patty, you should hang out a shingle giving relationship tips. You told me not to be needy, or clingy. Just to be so good she couldn't forget me. I did that as best I could. And in the end, in spite of serious competition, she chose me." Jake felt a little guilty over Alika. *Poor guy had lost his arm as well as his heart.*

"She almost picked another guy over *you*, Jake? Who is this woman?" Patty laughed. "Not that you're hot stuff or anything, bro."

"Sophie is unique. One in a million, truly. And I'm not the only one who thinks so." Even with Alika laid up and out of the picture, Jake couldn't rid himself of the feeling that Sophie might dump him at any moment. Just the thought made him clench his hands on the steering wheel. "She's still tough to pin down. She wouldn't agree to move in with me. Right now, I am shopping for two of everything for our apartments, which I think is stupid. But I respect the lady's need for space, and I'm taking no for an answer. For the moment." Jake cleared his throat. "On the same subject. I need a little more of that solid gold sisterly counsel. Things have been tricky with her. It seems like we take one step forward and two steps back at least half of the time. But she finally told me some of the reasons she was having difficulty being more open with me, and I thought we had a breakthrough. And then the very next day, I peeked into her back-pack...and saw a pregnancy test."

"Jake!" His sister's voice was a cross between a squeal of joy and one of panic. "Cardinal rule—never look in a woman's bag!"

Jake winced, shutting his eyes. "I know it was wrong."

"Geez. You can't possibly tell her you saw it."

"But don't I deserve to know? I mean, if she's pregnant...isn't it my baby, too?"

The line buzzed with Patty's silence, and Jake squirmed.

This was one of those tricky areas where he felt totally out of his depth with women. Even though his sister was pregnant with her first baby and happily married, Patty felt strongly about a woman's right to choose, that her body was her body. All of those issues seemed clear in theory, but not so much when they came down to actual fact. Because the thought of the woman he loved being pregnant activated feelings in Jake that felt primitive, intense, and urgent, way larger than the finer points of women's political rights.

Jake struggled to find words. "I just want to help. Take care of Sophie. Make sure everything is okay. Kill anybody who might hurt her. Or the baby, if there is one. I don't know how to talk about this." He pushed a hand impatiently through his hair, tugging on it as he stared out of the parked SUV's windshield. "Sophie not telling me about the pregnancy test feels...terrible. It's like barbed wire wrapping around and around, digging into me no matter which way I move. I don't know why she won't talk to me about it. And, the fact that she hasn't freaks me the hell out."

"Jake..." His sister sighed his name out on a long breath. "Sadly, I can see it from both of your points of view. She's probably way more freaked out than you are and has no idea what to do. She may even need more time to work up the nerve to take the test and find out for sure; she's probably still just hoping that nature will take its course and the whole thing will go away." Patty paused as if considering what to say. "If this woman isn't ready to move in with you, she certainly isn't ready to think about having a baby with you."

His sister's words, even softly spoken, still felt like a stab to the chest. Jake massaged that left pec, pressing hard on the source of his pain. "Don't hold back, Patty. Give it to me straight."

"That's why you called me, big brother. Even when Matt and I were talking about kids, and had gone off birth control... Getting pregnant was still a big deal. I didn't want to tell him at first. Didn't want to get him involved, excited, invested. Didn't want to have to deal with him and his feelings, too, when I was confused and conflicted myself. Telling him felt like too much." Patty sighed. "And my situation is ideal for having a child. We're married, committed to each other, financially solvent, even planning to have a family. And still it was scary to tell Matt. Hoping he'd be happy about it. Not sure what I would do if he wasn't. And scared as hell, myself, about what we were getting into."

"I guess I understand." Jake leaned his forehead on the steering wheel. "It still feels like she doesn't trust me."

"You have to be patient. I can't imagine what it must be like for your girlfriend. What she must be going through right now."

His girlfriend.

That phrase really had a nice ring to it, coming out of his sister's mouth.

He wouldn't mind hearing Patty say Sophie was his *fiancée*.

Or better yet, his *wife*.

Heat broke out under Jake's shirt, making it cling with nervous sweat. He looked up at the banyan tree sheltering their new apartment building. Mynahs were already roosting in its branches, chattering loudly. "What do you think I should do?"

"I thought I told you. Do nothing. Say nothing. And, when she tells you, whatever she tells you, you need to be there for her. She's got a hell of a lot more at stake than you do."

"I've got some skin in this game, too," Jake muttered. "Literally."

"That's true. You did donate sperm—the fun part, as they say." Patty's tone was dry. "But it's Sophie who's going to carry the child. Sophie who will have her health and her work impacted. Sophie who will live with whatever decision she makes about this baby for the rest of her life. Not you."

"I wish she would just tell me. I wish she would just let me help!" Jake's voice had risen, his fists had clenched. Frustration and helplessness were a ripe scent filling the cab of the SUV as he sweated with stress in the humid Hilo afternoon.

"It's hard to respect another person's privacy and right to choose," Patty said softly. "But if you love her, you will find a way to do that. Otherwise, from the things you've told me, this could be the way you lose her."

Jake breathed noisily, trying to get a grip on his emotions. "I'm a bull in a china shop with this stuff, Patty."

"That's why you have me, bro. There's hope for you, yet, because you're smart enough to call me and try to get this right."

CHAPTER EIGHTEEN

SOPHIE PLUGGED the external drive Pim Wat had given her into one of the computers Connor had had set up in the newly created "lab" room of their Security Solutions office. That the drive wasn't password protected spoke either to Pim Wat's ability to guard it, or to the Yām Khûmkạn's incompetence.

The information was simple: a couple of cloud storage sites on the dark net, one Tor website, and contact information for the agency's current tech. Sophie reached out to the tech contact, Leni Keng, on encrypted email, then opened up the website.

There was nothing to the site but a black background and the agency's name in Thai. Sophie had not uncovered it during her previous searches for the clandestine organization. When she clicked into the entry portal, it consisted of a downloadable PDF that was to be completed and mailed to an anonymous drop address listed on the form. The page was a recruitment portal for the Yām Khûmkạn.

Who received those recruitment applications and screened them? Was it this Keng character? Checking the information requested on the form certainly needed to be done, at least in part, online.

She needed to get on the same page with whoever was the Yām Khûmkạn's system admin. It was clear that the agency was trying to stay completely offline, but that was nearly impossible in this day and age. Sophie sent another encrypted email to Keng.

She then searched Interpol for anything to do with the organization. She'd heard from Pim Wat that Yām Khûmkạn agents' names were being released to the international police agency—but the Interpol site yielded nothing she could associate with the clandestine group without the operatives' names, and that information had not been provided on the data drive.

Sophie opened the cloud storage and found nothing but supply lists that appeared to be associated with the training temple. The whole mission and what Pim Wat wanted from Sophie were still hard to discern, and so far, none of the information had shed any further light.

Essentially, the stick drive contained nothing of any real value.

Sophie sat back in her chair. What was Pim Wat's real game? Was this a test of some kind?

She leaned forward and activated DAVID to search for more intel on the Yām Khûmkạn. She had done this before, but perhaps something new had shaken loose. She could also use DAVID to develop confidence ratios regarding related patterns of crime, but there was nothing to compare at the moment.

The Data Assessment Victim Information Database, Sophie's rogue information gathering program, sifted for intel based on keywords. She inputted several obvious ones and set it to combing the Internet for information on Keng and Pim Wat, as well. Information was power, and she just didn't have enough to even navigate.

Until Sophie heard back from Keng, there was little she could do. It was time to go "home" to her new apartment and move in. Jake had texted her that he was already there, unloading and setting up the basics he'd purchased with the stipend Connor had issued them.

SOPHIE PULLED up at the apartment building, scanning the nondescript parking lot with its coral stone wall buried in vines, a lone plumeria tree struggling for sunlight in the shade of a banyan overshadowing it. Three stories of industrial beige concrete block with exterior stairs and walkways, the edifice didn't send an affluent message—but Sophie liked the open lawn fronting the building and the ocean view facing Hilo Bay.

She texted Jake that she'd arrived as she took the stairs, supporting her sore ribs with a hand, and smiled to see Ginger and Tank galloping toward her down the open walkway. "Loosed the hounds, I see," she said, as Jake approached.

"They've been cooped up all day, and we need to put together the furniture I bought. Brought in all the stuff with the super's help."

"Thanks, Jake." Purchasing and hauling the furniture for two apartments up several flights of steps seemed to have wilted Jake's usual insouciance; he looked tired, his eyes iron-gray, his mouth a stern line. Sophie patted the dog's heads, and with one on either side of her, followed him to the doorway of her new apartment. "This is quite a project."

"Not that bad. I'm almost done here, then I'll go work on my place." Jake had purchased a metal-framed futon that made into a queen size bed, a desk and office chair, some bags containing bedding, and appliances still in their boxes in the kitchen. The metal parts of the futon were spread out on the carpet carefully, along with a battery-powered screwdriver. Jake knelt, picked up the schematic, and continued with his assembly.

Sophie shooed the dogs away from his carefully laid out diagram and walked across the living room area to the sliding glass door. Out on the deck, she leaned her arms on the railing and took a few deep breaths of the salty air wafting off of Hilo Bay. Late afternoon sun gilded the ripples on the ocean's surface with a shine like fool's gold. "I like this place much better by day. Being able to see the ocean is lovely."

Jake grunted, and she turned to peer at him. Focused on his

project, his big shoulders bunched as he secured a rod to a section of curved metal piping. Jake seemed completely absorbed.

Sophie went on. "I think I might like the bed, since it doubles as a couch, left out here in the living room so I can look out the window at the ocean during the night."

"I thought you wanted the extra room." The drill whirred. "And liked your blackout drapes."

"I want to try something different." And maybe she would need the extra room—*for the baby.*

Sophie's stomach roiled at the thought, but she breathed through it. Psychosomatic, that's what this was. Just thinking about being pregnant was making her have all the symptoms.

Sophie walked into the kitchen and began unboxing an electric teakettle, noticing the already assembled desk and office chair in the bedroom. She could work in there with her laptop. *Perfect for now.* "Is the internet hooked up yet?"

"Yep."

"Oh, good. Thank you." Sophie unpacked the basic kitchen supplies and stowed them in Formica cupboards, feeling a pang of regret for the soulful treehouse she'd lived in so briefly. This conventional apartment was a big change from that—but still an upgrade from the motel they'd been in for the last weeks.

Jake was soon done with the assembly and they moved the futon couch/bed to where Sophie wanted it, close to the sliders so she could look out at night.

"I've got to get my place set up." Jake headed for the door, all business.

"All right." Sophie watched him go, frowning. *Did he want to spend the night together?* Eat dinner together? He'd made no mention of it, and her stomach growled.

She usually let Jake decide what they were eating and where, but it would be a relief to be able to fix some food that wasn't from a restaurant. Jake deserved a meal after all his hard work.

Sophie made up the futon bed. The dogs had fallen asleep in the bedroom, snuggled up together, so she left them there and went back to the motel, packed her things and checked out, and drove to the market. She bought tea, vegetables, meat, rice, yogurt, eggs, and other basics. She paused as she was putting a six-pack of beer in her cart—and then took it back out.

No more drinking until she knew one way or the other about being pregnant. She had to get that test out of the way!

Back at the apartment, Sophie unpacked the groceries and laid out the ingredients for a vegetable and beef stir-fry. She loaded brown rice in the brand-new cooker Jake had bought—*so thoughtful.* He'd noticed that rice was a staple of her diet.

Jake would be a good father. Sophie felt sure of that.

But would Sophie be a good mother? With her depression? With her history of abuse? With the way her mother was? And what about the things the baby might have been exposed to already, given her crazy lifestyle?

Questions burst across her brain as her hands moved, seemingly disconnected from her body, measuring the rice, adding water, closing the lid, plugging in the machine.

Sophie removed the pregnancy test box from her backpack and stood staring at it. If only Marcella were here to support her through this moment...*and what would Sophie do if she were pregnant? It would change everything.*

Her pulse sounded like surf in her ears. She felt dizzy.

The door opened. "Sophie? You're back..." Jake's words died as his gaze fell on the small white box in her hands. "What's that?"

"A pregnancy test." Her voice sounded completely calm and normal even as her vision got spotty. She forced herself to breathe. "I'm late on my period."

His eyes widened. "Are you..."

"I don't know. That's why I have to take this." A bubble of hysterical mirth emerged in a squeaky giggle. "I'm so scared."

"Oh, Sophie." Two strides, and Jake had her in his arms—that warm, solid place where she could lay down her burdens. "You should have told me."

"I couldn't." She shook her head, rubbing her face back and forth against his shirt front, snuggling into him deeply. He'd showered and changed; he smelled of lemony aftershave and clean male. "I'm not ready to know yet, myself. But then I went to buy beer, and I decided I have to know."

"Beer as decider. I totally get it."

She snorted a laugh into his shirt. "Okay. I'm glad you're here for this." She detached herself. "The moment of truth."

He held her by her arms. "Whatever happens, I'll be there for you."

"Even if you're not the father?" Sophie clapped a hand over her mouth. *She hadn't meant to say that!*

Jake's face went pale. The light died in his eyes, leaving them the color of ash, and his features seemed to sharpen. He let go of her and stepped back.

"Who else did you sleep with? Alika?"

"Yes." Just a whisper, a trickle of sound. "It happened before we were exclusive. The night Alika and I were shot at, and I hid in his hotel room." Memories flooded her. "We didn't use protection."

"And *we have* been using protection, so there's a good chance it's his." Jake's expression had changed again. She was now looking at his combat face: remote, focused, his eyes steely, giving nothing away. *The face of a Special Forces killer.*

Sophie heard herself babbling. "But condoms. You know they don't always work…and we haven't been careful, either. I assumed I was barren, because Assan never got me pregnant in spite of years of trying. It never crossed my mind this could actually happen. I know it was stupid…" Sophie could feel Jake shutting down even as she gazed into his eyes, and it stole her breath. *She'd always known he'd take involvement with Alika as a betrayal.*

"Maybe this is just a scare," Jake said. "Maybe you *are* barren."

"Maybe I am." *Barren.* The word shouldn't hurt, but it did, and always had. Where was the softness she'd come to expect when Jake looked at her?

"Well, go find out." He turned Sophie and gave her a little push toward the bathroom door. "We need to know."

Sophie stumbled inside, swallowing sobs she didn't want to let out in front of him.

CHAPTER NINETEEN

JAKE STOOD outside the bathroom door, breathing hard, willing his heart rate to come down, his fists to unclench. He could hear Sophie's muffled crying through the closed door. He could picture her burying her face in a towel so he wouldn't hear. The sound physically hurt him—but the icy blade of betrayal slicing into his heart hurt worse.

She'd cheated on him and the baby wasn't his.

The pain was terrible. He'd rather be shot or tortured than feel this way; he was shocked at how quickly he'd been able to create a fictional family life with Sophie, how attached he'd become to his imagined child, just from knowing she had that pregnancy test in her pack.

He was supposed to see this some other way—supposed to be mature about it. Understand that they hadn't been exclusive when she slept with Alika. But jealousy and possessiveness and betrayal churned in his gut, anyway. *She knew he had a thing about cheaters and liars because of his dad being such an asshole...*

The dogs ambled out of the bedroom. Tank pressed his forehead against Jake's thigh in a comforting gesture, and Jake fondled the dog's ears instinctively. Gradually the warmth of the animals pressing against his legs calmed him. He walked to the sliding glass door, and out onto the deck.

His sister Patty's voice echoed in his mind: *"How you handle this could be the way you lose her."*

But maybe he didn't want to be with Sophie after all.

She didn't love him like he did her. And to take on another man's baby? *But maybe it was his.* He'd have to find out.

Patty was right. He should have run from this relationship when he had the chance.

Jake turned at the sound of the bathroom door opening. He hurried back as Sophie emerged, her face puffy and tear-stained.

"I'm pregnant." She held up a plastic wand. A thin blue line showed on it.

Their gazes locked. Jake couldn't think of what to say, and it appeared, neither could she. Suddenly Sophie's eyes rolled back, and she crumpled, so quickly he almost didn't catch her in time. Jake lowered her limp body gently to the carpet. He patted her cheek. "Sophie? Soph! Wake up."

She was unresponsive, her skin sallow and sweaty. He grabbed her wrist, felt for a pulse. Her heart rate was rapid and weak. "Sophie. Wake up." Was fainting part of pregnancy? Or was this situation just too stressful? Seeing her like this gutted him.

The dogs crowded around, whining and trying to lick Sophie's face and arms.

Jake yelled at them. "Go!" He pointed to the bedroom and the two obeyed, whimpering in protest. He jumped up and tore open one of the brand-new rolls of paper towels, dampening a handful at the sink, and ran back. He knelt and lifted Sophie into his arms, swiping at her face. "Wake up, Sophie, damn it."

Her eyelids fluttered and he set the paper towels aside. She turned into him with an inarticulate moan, clutching his shirt. "Jake..."

Relief that she was okay felt heady. He closed his eyes, savoring the feel of her in his arms, crushing her close. For a second it felt like they were together again, and nothing had changed.

Maybe it hadn't. Maybe the test was wrong. Maybe he hadn't heard her tell him she'd slept with Alika.

And then suddenly, Sophie stiffened, obviously remembering. She wrenched out of his arms and crab-walked backward away from him. She cupped her cheeks with her hands, her eyes huge. "Oh, no. I'm pregnant!"

"Yes, you are." Jake gazed at her, feeling dead inside. "We need to find out who the father is."

Sophie's full mouth tightened. Her amber-brown eyes heated. "So, you didn't mean it when you said you'd be there for me no matter what."

"I don't know." The words rolled out of his mouth to drop to the floor between them like stones. "I think some space to consider all options would be a good thing."

"If you're hinting that I would get rid of this baby because it's inconvenient—that is not an 'option' I would consider." Sophie's eyes blazed.

"That's not what I'm saying. It's your body and all that." Jake stood. He had to get away, consider *his* choices, and try not to make the situation any worse while he did so. "We should find out who the father is and go from there. I really do need some space right now." He snapped his fingers. "Tank! C'mon. We have our own place to go to."

Tank just stared at Jake from beside Ginger in the bedroom doorway. Jake walked over and grabbed the big pit bull's collar, hauling him toward the door. "You let me know how you want to go about the paternity test—I'm the first to admit I have no idea what to do next. I'll see you at work in the morning."

Jake dragged his reluctant dog out of the apartment and shut the door on the sight of Sophie's stricken face.

CHAPTER TWENTY

Sophie locked the door behind Jake, leaning against it, hearing his footsteps retreat on the walkway outside.

Despair rose like swamp water, welling up inside her. "Hello, depression. My old friend."

But she couldn't give in to that familiar deadening dark. Much as Sophie wanted to just lie down on the floor and wallow in self-pity, she couldn't. She had another life to care for now, and she'd just fainted—probably because she hadn't eaten for most of the day.

From here on out, self-neglect had to end. Her baby needed food, even if that was the last thing she was interested in right now.

Ginger whined, looking anxiously back and forth between the door and Sophie. "No. Tank is with Jake. I'll fix you some dinner," Sophie told the Lab. Her dog needed her, too.

Being needed helped her keep going.

The insight burst across her brain. From now on, she'd always be needed by someone very close to her. Was she up to the task? Could she be a better mother than hers had been? Surely, she could. She was no Pim Wat, filled with selfish, hidden agendas, using her depression as a smokescreen.

The smell of brown rice cooking penetrated Sophie's nostrils as she opened the bag of dog kibble she'd brought from the motel. She breathed through her mouth to avoid the weird combination of the smell of cooking rice and dog food. *Smells were definitely more intense.*

She poured a pile of kibble onto one of the paper plates Jake had brought.

Ginger fed, Sophie proceeded to chop the vegetables for the stir-fry she had meant to cook for both her and Jake for dinner—the first time she'd fixed a meal for Jake in her living space. She had been planning to surprise him by actually doing something for him; Jake more than deserved it.

Tears stung Sophie's eyes as she tossed the vegetables and beef into the hot oil of the big Teflon pan he'd bought her.

What would she do without Jake's unstinting support, his help, his hugs?

She swallowed the lump in her throat. Selfish to wish he would just understand how the situation had happened, selfish to wish he'd meant what he said about supporting her. She'd always known he struggled with jealousy, with wounds inflicted by his faithless father. This had to be hurting him deeply.

And what about Alika? What should she do about finding out if he might be her child's father? "What a can of worms," Marcella's voice said in her head.

Sophie's appointment with Dr. Wilson was still days away, but she could talk to Marcella. *Marcella would know what to do.*

Sophie put in her Bluetooth and called her friend as she finished up the stir-fry.

"Hey girl! This is so weird. I was just getting ready to call you. Friend ESP or something." Marcella's cheerful voice made the lump in Sophie's throat thicken.

She turned off the flame under the pan and cleared her throat. "Marcella. I'm in deep kimchee, as Lei would say."

"Oh, no, what now?" No matter how many dangerous situations

Sophie got into, Marcella's response was always immediate, heartfelt compassion.

The tears filling Sophie's eyes overflowed. "I'm pregnant."

Dead silence.

"Marcella? Are you there?"

"I'm here. Sorry. It's just…wow! Oh my God!"

"I know."

"What are you going to do?"

"Give birth to the baby." Heat flushed Sophie's body and her spine stiffened with resolution. She set down the bamboo spatula and walked back and forth, sorting her thoughts. Ginger's brown eyes tracked her anxiously, and she trailed a hand over the dog's head in reassurance. "I know it's a terrible idea, in practical terms. A baby will interfere with my work. I will have to make a whole lot of changes. It will be challenging to get through all of this as a single mother. But this is my child. I've always loved kids, and never thought I could have any. This is a secret longing of mine. A dream I never imagined would come true."

"Good." Marcella's voice firmed. "Good, Sophie. Because I can only imagine what would happen with your depression if you…got rid of it. You'd hate yourself. For all the reasons you just told me you want to keep it. I know you well enough to know that."

"Yes." Sophie's stomach rumbled, and she returned to the kitchen. "Do you mind if I eat while we talk? I fainted after I told Jake. I've gone too long without eating."

"You fainted? You told Jake? Oh man! What did he say?" Marcella's voice had gone high-pitched and her rapid-fire questions made Sophie dizzy again.

"Jake said he needed some space. And he left." Sophie carried her bowl of rice and stir-fry across the room. "He was upset that he might not be the father."

"Oh crap, Sophie! You must have told him about that time with Alika. I knew that was going to blow up… I need some wine." Sophie could hear her friend padding across the wooden floor of the little cottage outside of Honolulu that she shared with her fiancé, Marcus Kamuela. Being able to picture their pretty, tidy little home almost made Sophie smile.

Sophie carried her food outside and sat cross-legged on the textured floor of the deck. Ocean-scented air off of Hilo Bay wafted up to cool her hot face. She took several bites of the stir-fry with rice. She enjoyed the tastes and textures of the food, the way her stomach immediately settled.

Savoring little things, when big things were too much, was something she could always return to.

"I've got my wine and I'm on the back porch. Ready to really dig into this deep kimchee," Marcella said. Sophie heard the creak of her friend's chair.

"And I'm on the deck of my new apartment. Eating. It's a nice place to be. Thank you for being someone I can always call, no matter what."

"You got it, girlfriend. Now, back up the bus and start at the beginning. When did you first suspect you might be pregnant?"

Sophie told her friend about the session with Dr. Wilson and the series of events leading to the current situation. "I think Jake would be happy if he knew the baby was his. But he's having a tough time with the fact that I was with Alika even once, though Jake and I weren't officially together then."

"Yeah. I saw that coming," Marcella said ruefully. "Jake's one of those old-fashioned alpha males. Territorial. Did he smash anything?"

"No. He seemed sad. Like he was trying really hard not to say the wrong thing, even though he couldn't say what I wanted to hear." Sophie blinked stinging eyes. "I hate to hurt him, and I don't want to go through this without him."

"Sounds like you might have fallen in love with him somewhere along the way. That wouldn't be a bad thing."

"I don't know. Maybe I have. I just know I can't stand the thought of him hurting, and I miss him when he's not here." Sophie had finished her bowl of food, and she set it aside. She shut her eyes. "I need to find out who the father is, but I'm scared to know."

"Of course you are. Ugh, Sophie, I'm so sorry about this. What a can of worms."

Sophie smiled. "That's so funny. Earlier when I was thinking about this I heard your voice in my head say just that, about the can of worms. But don't be sorry. I'm actually happy about the baby, even if the circumstances aren't ideal." Sophie's hands had come to rest naturally against her abdomen; the tiny life beneath her touch seemed to flicker within like a star's faraway light. "There's a noninvasive blood test that can be done to determine paternity. The tricky thing is, everyone involved needs to submit blood. And that means I have to talk to Alika. Tell him I might be pregnant. Ask him to take the test." Her stomach gave a sudden lurch and she swallowed. "And I have been avoiding him. Haven't seen or spoken to him since the bomb."

"I know. And I know it's been eating you up."

"That's exactly the feeling. The guilt just seems to gnaw at me." Sophie rubbed her eyes. "I was planning to write Alika a letter. Dr. Wilson's idea. But then this week got so crazy that I never found the time. Do you think I should just go to Kaua'i and see him?"

"Yes, I do. Get everything out on the table in person."

"And I need to tell Connor, too."

"Why?" Marcella's voice had gone hostile. She was the only person besides Sophie who knew Connor, the Ghost, was also Sheldon Hamilton. Marcella had tried to bring him down through the FBI and failed to make anything stick.

"I owe Connor so much…"

"You don't owe him shit. He's your boss. You work for him, that's all. And you're an independent contractor; you can leave anytime."

Sophie sighed. "You know that's not all there is to it."

"You don't still have feelings for him, do you?" Marcella

sounded horrified. "Never forget what he put you through. That funeral! I was there. I saw what he did. What he is."

"I don't forget. But I do forgive. It's complicated. He's my friend. He understands me like no one else does. I don't have any secrets from him."

Marcella snorted. "You didn't sleep with Connor, too, did you?"

"Ha. No. Not since his fake funeral. I'm over him that way. But he is not over me. He told me so clearly." Sophie listened to the shrill song of the coqui frogs and the gentle shush of the water against the seawall below the building. "I am working closely with Connor on a confidential project. He will have to know eventually, and I'd rather it was sooner than later, in case it causes problems."

"Brace yourself for more fireworks," Marcella said darkly.

"Ugh! I'm tired from all of this drama. I'll keep you posted on any new developments."

"You'd better. Are you telling everyone your baby news? Or am I sworn to secrecy?"

"I'd prefer you kept this news quiet until…things settle a bit. It is early—perhaps something will go wrong with the pregnancy, and I want to get the paternity question answered and out of the way. Then I can talk more openly about it. Tell my father." Sophie shook her head. "I don't know what he will say."

"Frank will just be worried about you, Sophie. And he'll want to be involved."

"Fussing like a mother hen. I can hear him now. He will want to know everything."

"Exactly." Marcella yawned. "Let's both get some sleep. See what life brings in the morning."

Sophie said goodbye. She rinsed her dishes, brushed her teeth, turned off the lights, and snuggled into her new bed.

She couldn't help remembering the sight of Jake assembling the bed for her, his absorption in the project. His thoughtfulness was so endearing.

Fresh tears filled her eyes. *There was no way out of this situation that didn't hurt someone.*

Lying on her side, the glass slider open with just a screen, she looked out at the moon on the ocean. She listened to the frog chorus, and the wind in the banyan, and the sound of the ocean. She stroked her abdomen with her fingers, tracing the tattoos in Thai that encircled her navel: *love, joy, bliss.*

Perhaps those things were coming to her in a surprising new way.

Ginger hopped up onto the bed stealthily. Sophie pretended not to notice as the dog curled once and pressed her warm bulk up against Sophie's back.

She still missed Jake, but Ginger was warm, too. Sophie fell asleep, one hand resting on her belly.

CHAPTER TWENTY-ONE

Day Four

Connor pushed open the heavy metal door of the jet as Sophie arrived for a morning meeting. Her eyes were puffy. Her short curls surrounded her face in a frizzy nimbus, and an ashy cast to her skin indicated stress. She was clearly upset about something.

"Pim Wat's flash drive is a waste of time." Sophie smacked the item in question into Connor's hand. "I don't know how to move forward on this situation with the Yām Khûmkạn."

"Come get settled. Have some tea."

"Perhaps another cup would be all right." Sophie slid into the jet's dining area, pulling a computer tablet out of the small backpack she carried everywhere. "I'm cutting down on caffeine."

Connor put on the automatic kettle and measured the loose leaf tea they both liked into a hand thrown clay pot he'd picked up in Japan. He glanced over his shoulder and watched as Sophie's long, golden-brown fingers flew over a wireless keyboard she'd connected to the tablet. "The Yām Khûmkạn's tech contact Leni Keng has responded to my email. I'm telling him I need more information than

Pim Wat provided. I don't even know what she truly wants me to do at this point."

"What happened last night?" Connor cocked his head. "You look like you've been crying."

To his surprise, Sophie's eyes filled immediately. She gave an audible sniff but didn't look up. She shook her head, and a tear spilled. She dashed it away. "We have business to take care of. We can speak later."

Connor frowned.

He returned to his own tablet, plugging in the drive to peruse the information Sophie's mother had provided. *Sketchy, at best.* Not enough to do anything with.

Could Pim Wat have some other agenda involving Sophie? Some other reason for trying to lure her to the Yām Khûmkạn's temple stronghold in Thailand?

"Leni Keng has provided me a video conferencing link," Sophie said. "I'd like to make this call here, so you can witness everything."

"Of course." Connor got up and poured the tea. He placed the matching cups and teapot on a tray and returned with them to the table. She would tell him what was really going on when she was ready.

Sophie activated software to record the video conference call. Connor slid a little closer to her when he resumed his seat so that he could see her screen but was still out of view of the camera.

Moments later, a young man's face appeared. Long hair in a ponytail and a plain white tee set off golden skin and Asian features.

As Connor had been concerned might happen, the two spoke rapidly in Thai, too quickly for his beginning language skills to follow. He caught about every third word. He watched Sophie's face, and the scrunch of her brows told him she wasn't pleased with what she was hearing.

Connor battled frustration at not understanding the language. *He'd run the whole thing through a translation program later and replay it as often as he wanted.* The two techs wrapped up the call, and Sophie punched the end button on her keyboard briskly.

She picked up her cup of tea and took a sip, then sat back and met his eyes squarely for the first time that day.

"I still don't know what my mother really wants, even after talking to Keng. The Yām Khûmkạn maintains a practically invisible digital footprint, and they have no plans of changing that. Keng told me that yes, there have been incursions, but the leaks were done the old-fashioned way: someone from within the organization outed agents' identities to Interpol. It had to have been done old-school, through in-person spying, or as a payoff for information. There is no roster of agents anywhere on a computer that Keng is aware of. The Yām stays off the grid. It's part of their defensive strategy."

"What is this job that she wants you to do, then?" Connor turned the handleless cup around and around in his hands. "I don't trust your mother as far as I can throw her."

"Yes. My mother is petite, but she would be difficult to hurl any distance. So that's a good analogy."

Connor flicked a glance at Sophie's face to make sure she wasn't teasing him, but her serious mien told him that she had, indeed, interpreted his turn of phrase literally. He suppressed a smile. He really loved her pedantic moments. "Pim Wat is playing a deep game."

Should he tell Sophie how the Ghost had been manipulating Pim Wat through selective information?

No.

Sophie would not like how he'd been using her mother to eliminate threats and enemies. Even though the kills Pim Wat had performed with the information he'd fed her showed the assassin's true colors, her actions also showed how far the woman would go to protect her offspring. Sophie might interpret that as love, when Pim Wat's murders were nothing but narcissistic, possessive self-interest.

Pim Wat wanted Sophie for some purpose not yet revealed.

They might have to go all the way to the stronghold in Thailand to find out what it was, and that wasn't a risk worth taking.

"We should get back to McDonald with this information from the stick drive and Keng. Tell him that we are currently stymied," Sophie said. "We've run into a wall, as they say."

"Nice turn of phrase." Connor refilled their teacups. "Let's give him a call on the secure number he provided."

Sophie nodded. Moments later, she set her phone on a stand between them. The CIA agent's voice fizzled slightly on the phone's speaker. "Devin McDonald."

"This is Sophie Ang, Mr. McDonald. You're on speaker. I'm with Mr. Hamilton of Security Solutions. We are in a secure location for this conversation."

"Good. What have you got for me?" McDonald didn't waste any time.

"I met with Pim Wat in a park yesterday, and she gave me a stick drive that was supposedly going to show me what the job for the Yām Khûmkạn was. There was hardly anything on it: a few read-only files stored in the Cloud, an application portal, and contact info for their tech agent. I just got off of a videoconference with that person. His name is Leni Keng." Sophie took a sip of tea and continued. "The tech confirmed that the Yām Khûmkạn has no centralized database and no online presence that the organization wants to maintain. He was confused as to why I was getting involved at all. I did not tell him how I came to have his contact information, only that I had been recruited by someone from the Yām to provide further tech support and wanted to get started." Sophie poured a little more tea. "My impression was that Keng was telling the truth. He honestly seemed to wonder what I could do or add to the current strategy he'd been tasked with—which was maintaining as little of a cyber presence as possible. In fact, the man said he spends the majority of his time tracking online mentions of the Yām Khûmkạn and removing them from the Web."

"Sounds fishy as hell." McDonald growled. "Do you think that there might be some other agenda going on? Maybe Pim Wat is off the reservation on this recruitment attempt and going it alone for her own reasons. You are her daughter, after all."

"What does that mean, 'off the reservation?'" Sophie's brows drew together. "Sounds like a racist phrase referring to Native Americans. Are you implying that my mother could be using the Yām Khûmkan for her own personal purposes?"

"Pim Wat wants you to go to the temple stronghold, and so do we. That's the logical next step in finding out more." McDonald sounded testy.

"Regardless, I won't go." Sophie said. When Connor glanced over at her, Sophie's arm muscles were tight as she crossed her fists over her waist.

"We need more from Pim Wat herself," Connor said. "Why she reached out to Sophie. Why she's been so persistent, but so uncommunicative about her actual purpose."

"Maybe the agency should grab Pim Wat. Ship her out to Guantánamo for a little questioning," McDonald said. "That can easily be arranged."

"Are you threatening my mother? Trying to gain my compliance by blackmailing me with her safety?" Sophie's voice trembled with outrage.

"I'm just saying that Pim Wat is behaving in a suspicious manner and would benefit from being formally interviewed. There is more than one way to skin a cat." The agent ended the call with a click.

"Skin a cat? That sounds terrible! *Son of a water buffalo! Foul stench of rats' entrails!*" Sophie wrapped her hands around her cup as if trying to warm them. "He threatened my mother with Guantánamo!"

"I told you the CIA did not have your best interests at heart," Connor said. "I have been waiting for them to play dirty pool, and it looks like McDonald just made his opening move." He reached over and covered Sophie's hand with his. "I know you don't want to go to the Yām Khûmkan temple, but it would be a fascinating recon. I could help keep you safe."

Sophie pulled away and stood up. "Keep me safe? Like you did when we were almost shot out of the sky in your helicopter?" She pressed a hand to her stomach, her fingers spread. "No, thank you."

Connor had never seen her make that gesture before. "What's going on, Sophie? Tell me."

Her eyes met his. "There's a very good reason why I don't want to go to the Yām Khûmkạn stronghold. I don't want to endanger my baby."

"Your what?" The meaning of her words refused to penetrate. "What baby?"

Sophie just stared at him, and the tiny circles her hand made against her abdomen drew his gaze. Realization burst over his brain in a heat wave of some deep emotion he could not put a name to. "You're pregnant."

"Yes."

"How far along?" Dizzying hope that she might be pregnant from their time together, that the child might be his, washed over him— but a second later reality swept that away. She would be well along in the pregnancy if that were true, and her belly still looked completely flat.

"I'm not sure. Eight weeks, perhaps." Sophie's cheeks had gone pink. Her tawny-brown eyes seemed to glow. "It is early yet, but I have to make lifestyle changes."

"You're happy about this?" Connor sounded incredulous, even to his own ears. It seemed impossible, but Sophie did appear happy about a circumstance that might be disastrous to her personally and professionally.

"It is not the best situation, and I was upset last night…but the longer I know about it, the better I feel about what's happened." Sophie sat back down, poured a little more tea. "I thought I could not have children. It was careless of me not to take enough precautions, but I find that I am indeed happy."

"And Jake? What does Jake think of becoming a father right now?" Connor's mouth tasted bitter as he forced the name out. *Jake.*

He wished he could hate that guy, but the man was likeable, good at his job, and clearly besotted with Sophie.

A shadow crossed Sophie's face. She picked up her cup and took a sip of the tea. "He is adjusting to the news."

"Is that why you were crying last night?" Devastated as he was, the thought of Jake rejecting the woman he loved and her child enraged Connor. "I'll kill him if he doesn't do right by you."

"You may not kill Jake, Connor. For any reason." *Always so literal.* But in this instance, Connor heard the command Sophie was issuing the Ghost. She got up, walked to the galley, and dumped the remaining liquid into the small steel sink. "This whole situation is not your business, really. I only told you so that you would understand why I am so adamant about not going to the stronghold. I didn't want to go before, but now I am certain it would be a dangerous move. I don't trust my mother, or why she wants me there. She might even have some new marriage alliance planned for me. There's nothing I would put past her."

"You are right not to trust Pim Wat. And how will she respond to knowing you're pregnant?" Connor frowned. He didn't have a good feeling—Pim Wat was unpredictable. She might hate the idea of being a grandmother, or love it. Either option could be threatening to Sophie.

Sophie turned to face him, hands supporting her on either side of the sink. "I don't want Pim Wat to find out. Ever. I don't want her around any child of mine." She blew out a breath. "I might as well tell you everything. Alika and I slept together during the time frame that might have led to the pregnancy. He also could be the father."

Jealousy stole his breath like a blow to the chest. Connor clicked his tongue sarcastically. "My, my. Sophie and her lovers. Quite a daytime reality show."

"Your judgment regarding my sex life is hypocrisy," Sophie said evenly. "How many women have you had in your bed? How many meaningless liaisons?"

"More than a few. None that I didn't take precautions with."

Connor regretted what he'd said. Women faced a double standard, and he'd succumbed to a crude inference. Unresolvable misery made every word feel heavy, every movement slow. "I'm sorry, Sophie. You should know…I haven't been with anyone since you, so it's hard for me to hear this." Connor turned away, looking out the window of the jet to get his emotions under control. "What's going to happen next?"

Sophie took his question literally. "I have a therapy appointment with Dr. Wilson scheduled for this afternoon. I also have to look for an obstetrics and gynecology physician and arrange for the paternity test and my own maternity checkup. Then I will make arrangements to go to Kaua`i and talk with Alika." She sighed. "I can only take one step at a time. The way forward seems uncertain and difficult."

A long silence passed as Connor struggled within himself.

Sophie needed a friend, someone to count on through all of this.

He'd told her once that love was wanting the beloved to have what they needed—even if that was someone else. Could he be that friend to her, continue to support her, even as she carried another man's child? It would certainly be easier for him if both Alika and Jake rejected her.

Connor allowed himself a moment of giddy hope: she would let him take care of her through this crisis. He would be by her side every step of the way. She'd not only forgive him, but fall in love with him again. He would adopt her baby and be her life partner. They would be a family.

But that dream wasn't likely to happen.

Alika and Jake loved her too, and whatever pique Jake might be feeling was likely to be short-lived, unless the child was Alika's. *But what if it was?* And she'd said she was done with Alika, regardless, that their lifestyles were incompatible…

There was no way to know what any of them would do.

He had to decide about his role with Sophie for himself, no one else, and not dependent on any other choice she made, either.

Resolved, Connor stood. He walked over and took Sophie's cold, limp hands. He rubbed her palms with his thumbs, willing warmth back into her, and held her apprehensive gaze as he did so.

"You don't have to go through this alone. No matter what happens, I'll help you. Don't bother making reservations for Kaua'i. I'll have Thom fly you over and bring you back when you're done talking to Alika and making any arrangements you need to. And whatever the medical things cost, don't worry. The company will pick it up. You and the baby will have the best care available."

Sophie's mouth opened. Her eyes filled. She crumpled forward into Connor's arms. She clung to him like a life raft. Her body shook with silent sobs.

It was disorienting to see her so vulnerable—even when he'd picked her up at the edge of death in the lava wilderness, she'd kept him at arm's length.

Protectiveness surged up in Connor as he patted her back, smoothed her hair, and let her ruin his immaculate shirt with tears. *Being needed was good enough for now.*

CHAPTER TWENTY-TWO

AFTER A SLEEPLESS NIGHT in his new studio apartment, Jake finished a hard run in the park with Tank to kick off the day. He dropped off the dog back at the condo and jogged two blocks to a gym he'd joined recently.

Now he bench pressed a barbell loaded with as much weight as he could take, heaving it up with animalistic grunts that expressed his feelings better than any words.

He didn't know how he was going to get past this.

Jake's logical brain argued that he and Sophie hadn't been officially together when she slept with Alika. Sophie had been honest, telling Jake that she still had feelings for the guy. He even knew the exact night it had happened: they'd been shot at, and she'd had to hide in Alika's hotel room. The whole thing was a natural setup. He shouldn't feel this way about it.

But that didn't change the sensation he'd had, a rending as if his heart had been ripped out when she told him that he might not be the baby's father.

The feelings of betrayal felt primitive and absolute, life-threatening, even. Just the thought of Sophie with Alika, of his rival's child in her womb, made him want to tear the world apart and set it on fire.

Jake pushed harder and faster on the bar.

Suddenly he reached the end of his reserves. The barbell trembled above him like a black guillotine. Spots danced in the corners of his vision. He simply couldn't get it back into its cradle. Maybe if he let go, it'd drop on him and end the misery permanently.

"Let me help." A familiar feminine voice. Felicia appeared in his line of sight. The grad student grabbed the weight beside his hands. Together, they were able to heave the massive thing back into its cradle.

Jake stared up at the receptionist in astonishment, trying to get his breath back as Felicia walked around to face him. She looked cute as sin, her blonde hair in pigtails, and she was wearing sexy little butt shorts and a tiny tank top that made the most of her twenty something assets. She wasn't moving off quickly, either; instead she stared down at him like she'd like to take a bite.

"Excuse me," Jake said loudly.

Felicia laughed. "Sorry. I was seeing if you were still alive, old man. Wanted to make sure you were breathing. Good thing you said something, or I'd have had to take a pulse."

They bantered in the office like that. She called him "old man" and he called her "babe," and other borderline inappropriate things. The flirtatious joking had been fun, a return to old patterns that he'd been slapped down for trying with Sophie. That Felicia seemed to enjoy it too had been a balm to his ego as he dealt with so many uncomfortable moments in his new relationship.

Which might be ending.

If Sophie was pregnant with Alika's baby, he honestly didn't know what he'd do. *But if it was his?* A whole different picture.

Somehow, he had to act normal and be supportive and he didn't know how.

Total avoidance seemed best until he could get in the right headspace.

The awful feedback loop of his thoughts played on repeat, as it had since he'd left Sophie's apartment the night before.

Jake realized he was staring at Felicia blankly.

"What? Have I got something on my face?" Felicia playfully crossed her eyes and stuck her tongue out, as if trying to lick something off her nose. She was freakin' adorable.

"Nope. You're good. But I'm not." Jake sat up and swung his legs over to sit on the side of the bench. He braced exhausted, quivering arms on his knees. "You came along just in time. I didn't even have enough breath left to call for help."

Felicia's blue eyes darkened with concern. "You know you should never let it go that far. I happened to notice you from across the room." She did a forehead smack. "I wasn't checking you out. I mean, I noticed you were in trouble."

"Thank God you did." Jake picked up a gym towel and wiped his face. "Pretty sad when a little girl has to save me."

"Hey. Who're you calling a little girl?" Felicia struck a pose, curling her arm. "I've worked hard for these guns. Besides, what've you got on there? Three fifty?" She peered at the stack of weights. "Anyone could get in trouble with that much weight."

"Three seventy-five. And yeah. I got distracted. Too caught up in my head." Jake took a sip of water from his squirt bottle. "Didn't know you came to this gym."

"Didn't know you did." Felicia glanced at the clock. "And we're both due in the office in forty-five minutes. You've got a meeting with Ilima Cruz, the lady in charge of the Merrie Monarch Festival. Sophie's supposed to be there too." She put her hands on her hips. "Do you know where Sophie is? I called her phone, but it went straight to voicemail."

"Yeah. She had an early meeting with Hamilton at the corporate plane. They have some special project they're working on." *And he shouldn't be jealous of that, either.*

Being in love with Sophie was making him crazy—when it wasn't the best thing in the world.

"Okay. Well, I'll see you at the office. Be sure to grab something to eat, old man. You need to keep up your strength." She bounced away across the gym.

*

ILIMA CRUZ WORE a Hawaiian-print flowered dress and her hair was braided like a crown. She swung a sandaled foot in an impatient arc as she waited in his office.

Jake had taken the time to run back to the condo for a quick shower and clean work outfit. His hair was still damp as he extended a hand to the lady, and then sat down behind his desk.

"Sorry to keep you waiting, Ms. Cruz."

"I'm here for an update. It seemed like your investigation was getting off to a good start, but we haven't heard anything since that first day when you came around to inspect the facilities and I met you on the grounds where the Festival is held." Her large brown eyes held impatience and something else—worry.

"You're right, you are overdue for an update. However, I'm not sure I should be reporting to you." Jake smiled, hoping to take the sting out of his words. "We report to our client."

"Tell me who your client is. You wouldn't tell me the day we met." Cruz's lips thinned and her brows drew together. "I'm in charge of the Festival. Everything that goes on regarding it is my business. I need to be kept in the loop."

Jake sat back and considered. "Let me call our client right now and see if we can just do an update via phone that you can listen to on speaker. We'll kill two birds with one stone. However, if the client is not comfortable with that, I will have to ask you to understand the confidentiality obligations we're under."

Cruz nodded her head stiffly. Jake heaved an internal sigh of relief and exited. He phoned Kim from the privacy of Sophie's office. She answered on the third ring, and once he had oriented her on the situation he said, "I'd like to give you an update with Ms. Cruz listening in on speakerphone, if that's all right."

"Sure, that would be fine—unless you've got anything indicating Ilima is involved?"

"Not so far."

"Then that's fine. You'll save me a phone call to her, anyway."

Back in his office, the women greeted each other as Jake put the phone on speaker and set it down. Cruz visibly relaxed in the chair in front of his desk, chatting with Kim, as Jake pulled out the case file. He flipped it open and proceeded when there was a break in the women's conversation.

"So. Our investigations have pointed us to the public relations and advertising firm, Coconut Wireless Advertising & Marketing, run by Penny Chang. We went to her office, posing as new clients looking for PR for an upcoming launch event and citing the sign outside of town at the airport as an example of what we were looking for. Ms. Chang was unhelpful." Jake set down the folder and put his fingertips together. "She cited various reasons why the Merrie Monarch Festival did not need to spend as much as we would have to as a startup. While not definitive, Sophie and I were left with the impression that Penny has justified herself in doing something else with the money given her to spend on the Merrie Monarch."

Cruz's dark brows lifted in surprise. "I know Penny. She always has to overcome being associated with her lousy relatives. That doesn't mean she doesn't run a good business. And really? That is all you were able to obtain as far as investigating? An impression?"

"No, there's more. Ms. Ang has the money trail mapped out, and Coconut Wireless appears to be the leak, but she will have to go over the details with you herself." Jake looked down at the file and pulled his thoughts together. "Our recommendation is that you ask for an accounting of the exact spend of the advertising budget, with accompanying documentation of where the money went. I think we have gone as far as we can with this. Doing anything else will likely alert others to our digging, giving whoever's involved time to cover their tracks."

"Do you think we have enough that we could go to the police?" Kim asked, her voice thin and fuzzy over the speakerphone.

"I'm sorry, Kim. It seems clear that the PR firm has had something, if not everything, to do with the missing money. But how exactly to proceed to track it down legally, let alone get the funds back, is another matter. I think you need to do the steps I recommended first. Perhaps there's some explanation we're not aware of. Your board, or other governing entity, should meet and discuss our findings. I'll type up a report for you, but I'll need a little time, and Ms. Ang's detailed input."

Cruz leaned forward and spoke into the speakerphone. "Kim, why don't you get hold of your rep from the Tourism Authority, and I'll contact the Festival bookkeeper and a couple of board members I know that can keep a confidence. Let's put our heads together and see if we can come up with a plan and try to get the money back privately. We don't want a public scandal that will make folks lose confidence in donating to and supporting the Festival."

"That sounds good," Kim replied. "There are still three weeks until the event. Maybe we can get the funds back and still put them to good use. If not, the money can roll over to next year." They wrapped up the call, and Jake escorted Ms. Cruz to the door.

When the event coordinator had been seen on her way, Jake turned back to face Felicia.

His erstwhile gym buddy had completely transformed herself. Her hair was scraped into a bun anchored at the back of her neck. She wore a calf-length, dirt-colored pencil skirt, clogs, and a man's white shirt that hung on her like a tent. Black glasses he'd never seen before hid her eyes.

"Going with the frumpy librarian look today, I see," Jake said.

Felicia shot him an annoyed glance over the top of the glasses. "I have to counteract the fact that you have seen me wearing pigtails and butt shorts, old man."

Jake advanced upon her desk. "An unforgettable sight, for sure. What've you got next for me?"

"We have a possible new client. Some dot-com guy, inventor of the MiracleApp, out in Hamakua. The dude works from home. He wants a new security system and likes the idea of the AI software. Wants to see if it will integrate with his app, which is some kind of smart home service aggregator. I have an appointment for you to go out and meet with him and do an assessment for a full system install, and whatever other services you can upsell—he seems a little paranoid, so you should have fun with that." Felicia handed Jake a file containing the intake forms and the address. "Probably take you a couple of hours. You'll still have time to type up the report for Ms. Kauwa and Ms. Cruz on the Merrie Monarch situation when you get back."

Gratitude warmed his gaze as Jake smiled down at Felicia. *Why couldn't he have fallen for a smart, nice, pretty, normal girl like her?* Life would have been so much easier. "Thanks, babe. Don't know what I'd do without you." He headed for the door.

"Don't call me 'babe.' Unless we're going on a date," Felicia called after him.

Jake closed the office door behind him and pretended he hadn't heard that.

CHAPTER TWENTY-THREE

SOPHIE LEANED her forehead against the window of the Hawaiian Air jet on its way to Kaua`i. Evening gilded the ocean as the plane took off from Hilo airport, and as always, Sophie enjoyed the sights of her new home island: the rising bulk of Kilauea off to one side, the smooth arc of Hilo Bay with its fringe of palms and banyans. The black lava teeth rimming the coast were softened by waves' foamy lace and a multiplicity of textured green foliage. As the plane rose, Sophie scanned the water for any sign of whales, but the cobalt ocean was opaque, marked only by the scuff of whitecaps.

Sophie accepted a plastic container of passion fruit, orange, and guava juice from the flight attendant. Shortly after she'd downed the sugary drink, energy surged back to fight the tiredness of a long, emotionally intense day.

She looked down at her phone, set to airplane mode, and scrolled through a series of texts she'd sent to make sure they sounded right. She'd agonized over the wording, the tone, not wanting to say too much or too little to each person.

To Alika: *"Hi Alika. I am so sorry to have been out of touch for so long, but there are things I need to speak to you about. I really need to see you in person; I am flying over today. I hope it will not be too much of an imposition if I rent a car and come out to your house. Please text me your address. Thanks!"*

To Felicia: *"Please block out my schedule for the next couple of days. I'm traveling on personal business. Mahalo!"*

And to Jake: *"I'm taking a quick trip to Kaua`i to meet with Alika about the paternity test. Can you take care of Ginger? I put her in your apartment. She was very happy to be with Tank again; I don't think we should separate the dogs anymore. No matter what happens with us, the dogs can both stay together at each of our places on alternating nights or something. I left a stick drive with the Merrie Monarch financial info report on the counter in your apartment."*
She'd debated about ending with a heart emoticon, but didn't want to pressure him, so she'd put a smiley face. Then that seemed too flippant, so she'd put a rainbow symbol instead. Texting was almost as hard as speaking to people in person.

To Connor: *"I can't thank you enough for your kindness and support this morning when I gave you my personal news. I really needed your understanding, and the hug, too. But, I just don't feel it would be right to take the company jet for such a personal errand, even though I greatly appreciate your offer to have Thom fly me. I'll be on Kaua`i for a few days meeting with Alika, so don't worry about where I am. Deepest friendship, Sophie."*

To Marcella: *"Dear BFF, I'm heading to Kaua`i to meet with Alika. Wish me luck and not to be too incoherent. I have no idea how much he will hate me because I never even acknowledged the loss of his arm. I wish I had you by my side so you could tell me what to say and how to act!"*

To her father, Frank: *"It's been a while, Dad, but this is just a note to let you know I'm still alive, all is well, and I'm flying to Kaua`i to meet Alika as you told me I should, to acknowledge the loss of his arm and other things. Thanks for always being there for me, and for always challenging me to do the right thing. I love you."*

To Dr. Wilson: *"Thanks, dear Dr. Wilson, for the session today, and for helping me see that I am in charge of my life, my body, and my choices. I don't need anyone to take care of, or rescue, me or my baby. I'm capable, I have money and friends, and whatever the men in my life think about me and my child, it's my opinion that matters most. Though there may be emotional pain ahead, I'm a survivor and I can handle it. I thank you for the extra-long session we had to sort all of this out, and I look forward to updating you on how my visit to Alika and the situation with how the paternity test go. Many thanks, Sophie."*

The session with Dr. Wilson had cemented her determination to see Alika and talk things through with him. She would always remember Dr. Wilson's kind, direct blue eyes as the psychologist listened to her outpouring while she described the last few days' events and her pregnancy news. They'd sorted through Sophie's fears about Jake, about facing Alika, and even the surprisingly unstinting support she'd received from Connor.

"In the end you don't need any of them. Not even your father," Dr. Wilson had said. "I don't think it will come to this, but it's useful for you to acknowledge that you may be the only person this child has, and if so, you can still do a great job parenting." Together they'd searched out various articles and resources for Sophie to study. "The most important thing is that you get calm and confident about your choice to keep the baby. Everyone else will settle down around that in whatever way they choose to, but ultimately you're not in control of their reactions—and you have to accept that, and be okay with yourself and your choice, come what may."

Sophie put her phone back into the travel backpack she'd packed with a couple of changes of clothes and other essentials, feeling calmer.

Maybe she'd only be on Kaua'i overnight, but it was better to be prepared. She leaned her head back against the seat and the tiredness that she'd read was such a part of first trimester pregnancy swamped her. She slept for the rest of the hour-long flight.

CHAPTER TWENTY-FOUR

Akane Chang loaded the hunting rifle, ramming in a shell and ratcheting it home. There was no point in getting some fancy sniper rifle; he already had a good pig-hunting gun in his personal arsenal, and the target wasn't far. He'd got a call from a friendly cousin telling him where to find that bitch investigator and her partner; taking them down was going to be so satisfying, the perfect way to announce he was back in town.

Getting back to the Big Island from Oahu undetected had been more of a challenge than Akane had anticipated. He'd called in many a favor to get here, finally hitching a ride on a third cousin's fishing boat and arriving at night. Many in the family were intimidated by Terence Chang's massacre of Akane's family, so he'd had to choose his contacts carefully.

Disguised as a fisherman, he'd visited the Chang's memorial park area. His family had all simply disappeared, so not so much as a plaque marked their vanishing. Akane had brought lei, one for each missing member, and he'd draped them along the top of the memorial wall where the ash cisterns were stored. He'd taken time to grieve alone.

Freakin' Terence had even shot Akane's mother! Who knew that poser with his hipster jeans had a heart of stone beating under his designer shirt?

Akane tried to imagine pulling the trigger on his closest family members. His brother Byron was the only one he'd have enjoyed killing, and Byron had been dispatched by the assassin he'd hired to replace Akane—a fitting irony.

His family's murders weren't even being investigated, because no one who'd witnessed the massacre was talking to the cops, and no bodies had yet been found. His contact in the Hilo PD told him that evidence planted at their homes indicated that they'd left on vacation.

What had Terence done with them?

His imagination tormented him. That Akane had so much experience making people disappear himself was insult added to injury, and solidified the rage burning in his chest.

Akane ground his teeth as he ran a rag over the gun and checked the sights. He'd broken into his parents' empty home to get the rifle. He'd seen a typed note left out for a house-sitting service. The note was supposedly from his mother, leaving directions on watering the plants. His parents' home had smelled fresh and aired, as if they'd return any minute.

He'd vomited from grief in their immaculate bathroom.

"Clever Terence. I'm saving you for last," Akane muttered. He propped the rifle on the windowsill, sighting down at the door of the business building that housed Security Solutions, directly across the street. "I'm starting here, with these rent-a-cops, and then I'll kill everyone you ever cared about. And when that's done, I'll cut you up alive and throw you to Pele to burn."

Terence would pay. *They all would pay.* Getting the tip about the location of the investigators' office had provided a good focus, an easy first target. He wouldn't even have to get his hands dirty—*he'd save that for later.* "Like shooting fish in a barrel. All I have to do is wait."

Akane pointed the rifle at the entrance to the building. He

propped a photo of the investigators that his cousin Penny Chang had provided him against the lamp on a side table near his chair. He would easily recognize that ballbuster Sophie Ang and her jock boyfriend Jake Dunn, but a visual aid never hurt. *Too bad he wasn't going to be able to rape the woman before he killed her.*

He was saving that personal touch for Terence's girl, Julie Weathersby.

Akane opened a bag of pork rinds and a Kona Brewing Company dark ale, and settled in to wait.

CHAPTER TWENTY-FIVE

JAKE CLATTERED RAPIDLY down the interior stairs of the Security Solutions office building as he usually did. He was already several steps ahead mentally as he pushed through the glass entry door and stepped outside the building, the file Felicia had given him tucked under his arm. The folder slid out and hit the sidewalk, scattering papers.

Jake bent to the side to retrieve it, and heard the sound of a rifle's report at the same moment a hot shock of pain bit the back of his calf.

Combat reflexes took over. He dove for cover as his brain scrambled to catch up: *who would be shooting at him?*

From behind an old blue Chevy Impala parked at the curb, Jake scanned the street, applying pressure to his calf.

Yep. He was shot.

Blood saturated his pants and warmed his hand as he continued to apply pressure to the wound without looking at it, his weapon in his hand.

People were going about their business on the busy thoroughfare only a block away and no further shots rang out.

Jake scanned the building across the street. His eye caught a flash, a glimmer of light on metal several floors up, just as the window of the Impala exploded above him.

"Shit!" Jake covered his head with his arms as safety glass showered him in a rainbow of sharp, jagged little cubes.

He fumbled his phone out of his pocket and called 911, barking out the street address and reporting that someone was firing at him from the building across the street. Someone else also must've called, because Jake could already hear the wail of sirens in the distance. He slid his phone back into his pocket despite the dispatcher's protests and squinted up at the window from where the shots had come.

No gleam of metal. No rifle barrel. *The shooter had pulled out.*

This was his chance. The perp was going to be long gone by the time the cops arrived.

When Jake stood up, pain hit him like a baseball bat. His head swam. Shock was setting in. He didn't need to examine the injury to know that it was just a through and through to the calf muscle.

That didn't mean it didn't hurt like a mofo, but he'd fought entire battles with worse.

Jake ripped off his black Security Solutions shirt and leaned down to tie it around his lower leg as tightly as possible. Barechested, gun drawn, he ran and hobbled as fast as he could across the road and into the building.

The apartment's entry foyer was unlocked, and he searched wildly for a set of stairs in the nondescript lobby with its wall of mailboxes. Spotting a door marked STAIRS beside the elevator, he paused to consider.

The car was descending, the lights changing above the door.

Maybe the shooter was coming right to him.

Jake took up a defensive position beside the elevator's entry, his weapon at the ready, and when a *ding!* announced the car's arrival, he brought the pistol down, covering the man getting off.

"Stop right where you are. Put your hands on your head."

The passenger exiting the elevator froze, his mouth open. He dropped a bag he was holding and put his hands on his head. Six feet in height, with gray hair in a ponytail, the middle-aged white male wore a really bad tie-dyed sweatshirt advertising a head shop.

"No gun violence!" Tie Dye yelled. "Get the hell away from me with that murder stick!"

Not his shooter.

Jake shoved the man forward out of the way and jumped inside the elevator. He hit the button for the fourth floor repeatedly.

Years of studying maps and floor plans for various missions had trained him to match locations with internal structures seen from different angles. An internal schematic of where the window was relative to Jake's current position stayed clear in his mind, and he watched the floors changing impatiently. The first rush of adrenaline was wearing off and pulsing pain had set in, a hot poker beating a tattoo on the back of his leg.

The fourth floor was dim and quiet. Jake flicked on a light switch, but the power was off. Drop cloths, paint buckets, and the dim shapes of equipment, told him that the floor was being remodeled. It appeared unoccupied at the moment—*ideal for the shooter.*

Jake ignored his calf dripping blood as he trotted lightly on the balls of his feet to the door that matched the window he'd spotted from the street below. He reached out from the cover of the wall to give the handle a quick twist, just to check if it was open, and the portal swung inward. Jake waited a moment for the rush of feet, the report of a gun, but heard nothing from inside.

He peered around the jamb into an empty, barely furnished apartment. A chair, nightstand and lamp were set up near the window. An empty beer bottle and an open bag of pork rinds gave testimony to the shooter's presence, but the brass from the rounds had been picked up.

The guy had probably been taking the stairs while Jake took the elevator.

He tried not to be too frustrated—it was a fifty-fifty gamble, one way or the other. Time to let the cops do their job. He looked down at the beer bottle. *Careless.* The shooter had picked up his brass, but likely left prints.

Jake called 911 again to inform the officers about his discovery.

He was told to wait for their arrival, and Jake was finally ready to sit down and take the weight off of his injured leg.

Then he called Sophie. The call went straight to voicemail. "Soph. Hey. I got shot in the leg across the street from our office building. It's not terrible, but I'm gonna need a hospital visit." His voice wavered as his gaze fell on the beer bottle. "Looks like the shooter left some evidence behind. I'm thinking it's Akane Chang. Call me. I need to know that you're safe."

He slid the phone back into his pocket.

The cops burst in, and all was chaos until he was able to establish that he was both the victim and the 911 tipster.

"Why didn't you stay in the street?" The uniformed cop holding a gun on him asked. "You probably scared the assailant off."

"The shooter took two shots and cut his losses." Jake said. "I would have caught him if I'd taken the stairs. Bag that bottle and check for prints."

The cop scowled. He flicked a glance at Jake's buff, naked torso. "Who do you think you are? Rambo? Shut up, *haole*. I'd still like to bring you in."

The EMTs had finally arrived, and by then, Jake was ready to let them strap him on a gurney and haul him away.

"Call Detective Freitan!" Jake yelled from the gurney. "Tell her to look for the bullet that got my leg over on the street by the Impala. You might be able to match it to a weapon in the system."

None of the local cops, eyeing him suspiciously as if he'd somehow brought this on himself, appeared inclined to listen.

Jake shut his eyes as he was wheeled onto the elevator he'd come up on, slightly alarmed by the amount of blood he'd trailed through the building. *That was going to be a bitch to clean up.* They'd probably send him a bill...

He must have passed out, because getting his pants cut off in the

Emergency Room brought him around with a groan. *Where was Sophie? Was she safe?*

"Who should we call for you, sir?" the intake nurse asked, pen poised over a clipboard as the tech yanked him to and fro, hacking at his bloody combat pants with a pair of shears.

"Call my office. Tell Felicia to notify our supervisor, Kendall Bix, on Oahu. And have her call Sheldon Hamilton from my company—he's the big boss, and he's on island." Jake's brain felt too fuzzy to recall the numbers, so he fumbled the phone out of his pocket and read them off.

"Any family to call?" The woman persisted. "You'll need someone to give you a ride home if you're not admitted."

"No family." Jake's belly tightened at the way the words sounded. *Sophie was the closest person he had to family.* "My relatives are on the Mainland. They can't help." He checked his phone again, and this time noticed a text from Sophie. She was on Kaua`i, and she'd left Ginger for him to care for in his apartment.

Sophie was talking to Alika. *Good.* She'd be safe, for the moment, away from here.

Jake tried not to imagine how that difficult talk was going. Was she even going to come back to the Big Island? Or would she just— stay with the guy? He hadn't given her much reason to return, and even with this latest crisis, he still wasn't sure how to move forward.

Better she left him now if she and Alika were having a baby together... Jake clenched a fist. Waiting to know something had never been so hard.

"You've lost a lot of blood in spite of this improvised tourniquet," the doc said, once the pants were out of the way and she was assessing the wound in his calf. "I'm going to need to stitch this up, and it's going to take a while. Need something for the pain?"

"Hell yeah. Bring on the meds." Jake shut his eyes and awaited blessed relief.

SEVERAL HOURS LATER, Felicia wheeled him out of the ER toward her car, a new VW Bug in bright blue with surf racks on top. "I can't believe you don't have someone else to call. Where's Sophie?"

"She had to go off island on personal business." Jake's head felt too heavy to hold up and his tongue was thick in his mouth. The doc had been on the verge of admitting him, but Jake had insisted on going home—the dogs were trapped in the condo. *He had to get back to them.*

He gave Felicia the apartment building's address, and soon she was helping him up the stairs and into the building, her petite frame wedged under his armpit, holding him up surprisingly well. Clearly the girl worked out a lot, as if her sexy shorts and strong arms hadn't already told him that.

"I need to get those crutches the doc prescribed," Jake murmured. He was so sleepy from the medication he could hardly keep his eyes open. "But first, I've gotta walk the dogs. They need to go out."

"Oh, now I know why you were so hell-bent on getting back to the apartment," Felicia panted, propping Jake against the wall of the rickety elevator and punching his floor's button. "Don't worry. I'll take the dogs out and run by the pharmacy and get your meds and the crutches, too." The elevator creaked as it slowly rose.

"Don't know what I'd do without you, babe." Jake's arm was still over Felicia's shoulder, and he kissed the top of her head. "My girl Friday."

"Don't call me babe, Jake." Felicia stiffened and pulled away to stand across the doorway from him. "You're with Sophie."

"I thought you liked being called 'babe,' sweetheart." Jake tried to enunciate.

"That was…before I knew you guys were together." Felicia's face was turned away. "I didn't mind then. I mind, now."

"I don't know if we're together. I don't know what's going on with Sophie. As usual. She's pregnant. It might be mine, it might be someone else's." Jake clapped a hand over his mouth. "Oops. Pretty sure I wasn't supposed to tell you. Meds talking."

"Oh my God!" Felicia's eyes were a very bright blue. "That's... wow. Tough stuff, Jake. I'm sorry you guys are going through that. Did she say what she's doing about the baby?"

"Yeah. She's keeping it. She's on Kaua`i telling the other guy to get a paternity test. I'm doing one too. Obviously."

"Obviously," Felicia echoed, her voice hollow. The elevator dinged as it reached Jake's floor, and Felicia hefted him out. She puffed as they staggered down the hall. Jake pointed to his door, and she used his key to open it.

The dogs, waiting on the other side, swarmed them. Jake batted at them with a hand, shooing them away. Felicia maneuvered him to the open, unmade futon bed parked in front of the sliders. A breeze blew in and cooled his hot face as he sat down. The room whirled around him, and spots danced in the corners of his vision. "Wow. I'm tripping on these meds."

"We should get those pants off you. They're cut to bits and covered with blood," Felicia said.

"Yeah. Don't worry, I don't go commando," Jake murmured. "Thanks, Felicia. You rock." Jake shut his eyes as she removed his wallet and weapon, unbuckled his belt, and helped him slide the pants, cut off above the knees, all the way off of him. The hospital had allowed him to wear the gown covering his upper torso out of the building, and Felicia removed that, too. She lifted his foot, encased in a structured boot, up onto the bed and tilted him back until his head hit the pillow.

"You going to be okay? I'm going to take the dogs out for a walk and then go get that stuff you need." Felicia's voice came from far above Jake, but he didn't open his eyes. He was just too tired to speak, and then he was gone.

CHAPTER TWENTY-SIX

Day Five

K AUA῾I had such a different feeling about it from the Big Island.

Sophie gazed out at the ocean from her little fourth-floor deck at the Hanalei Bay Resort. Surfers were clearly visible. A fresh wind stirred the palms and a nearby banyan tree; mynahs hopped on the mowed grass below the unit.

But there the resemblance to her ocean vista in Hilo ended. The view this resort faced was breathtaking, a triptych of rugged mountains and iconic headland. Active with wind and waves, Hanalei Bay was completely different from Hilo's sheltered calm. The ocean was bright blue and turquoise, dappled with greenish-brown reef, and surfers worked the right-hand break across from the river mouth.

Sophie closed her eyes and focused on her breathing, then went into her morning routine of sun salutations. Nausea plucked at the back of her throat, but she breathed through it, trying not to think of the upcoming meeting at Alika's house in Princeville, an exclusive ridge community above Hanalei Valley.

Showered, dressed, even wearing a little makeup, Sophie was soon on the road in a yellow Chevrolet rental to Alika's address. Her

TOBY NEAL

Mary Watson identity had felt like the right look to wear. She liked the swishy skirt and cream silk blouse that left her arms bare—cool and comfortable. Sophie felt pretty.

And after a brief, violent vomiting episode following her yoga practice, Sophie badly needed to feel pretty.

She battled a sense of déjà vu as she drove down a winding avenue to park in front of a mansion built of sienna-colored stonework, with a cobalt-blue ceramic tile roof that gleamed in the sun. This was the house and grounds she'd seen in a dream, flying over it in Alika's helicopter!

But she could swear she'd never seen even a photograph of it before. *How very strange.*

The hairs on Sophie's arms rose as she looked around at gracious, full-sized palm plantings that were still finding their roots with the aid of bamboo trellising. Beyond the house's bluff view, the swooping patchwork of taro fields and a sinuous green river down in the valley was set off by three peaked mountains.

A closed four-car garage gave no indication whether or not Alika was home, and Sophie wiped sweaty hands on her skirt as she got out of the car. She approached teak double doors with huge brass scrollwork handles and stood for a long moment on the flagstone step, her finger poised above the doorbell's button as she dug deep for the courage to ring it.

Before she could do so, the door swung open.

Esther Ka'awai gazed up into Sophie's surprised face. Alika's grandmother wore a casual house muumuu in floral fabric. Her long hair was down, a curtain of black and silver hanging to her hips. Her weathered brown face broke into a bright smile. "Sophie! I thought you might be visiting. It is so good to see you again."

Surprise and deep humiliation locked up Sophie's muscles, but her frozen posture didn't stop Esther from embracing her stiff body. "I am glad you finally came to see Alika. He is healing well but seeing you will no doubt speed things further."

Sophie ducked her head. "I am so ashamed that I never visited him in the hospital. I felt so guilty."

Esther patted her shoulder. "It's not me you have to apologize to. Besides, you are here now to make up for it." She held Sophie at arm's length. "I hear good things about your investigation into the disappearance of the Merrie Monarch funds. My *haumana*, Kim Kauwa, my student, speaks highly of your agency and your work."

Sophie nodded, relieved to be moving away from personal topics. "Yes. In fact, I left detailed information for an update for Kim and the Tourism Authority Board with Jake, my partner. But if you would like to hear some of that in person, I'd be happy to update you."

"No, no. Now is not the time." Esther pushed one side of the huge door wide. "*E komo mai!* Welcome. Make yourself at home, and I'll let Alika know you are here."

"Tutu." Alika's voice came from the other side of his grandmother. "I don't need you to be my butler."

"No such thing, mo'opuna. I know you were doing your exercises, and I wanted to say hello to Sophie myself." Esther's warmth, as she squeezed Sophie's arm, nearly brought tears so Sophie's eyes. The older woman left them standing facing each other.

Sophie assessed Alika. He had lost a good deal of weight since the bomb attack at Sophie's father's building, and his bold cheekbones stood out in sharp relief. He was paler and reduced in size from his usual muscularity, but he stood straight, brown eyes calm and steady. Sophie finally allowed her gaze to rest on what was left of his arm.

Severed above the elbow, the left side of him seemed unbalanced, asymmetrical. The stump was still wrapped in some sort of bandage. Sophie felt nausea roll through her belly.

Alika opened his arms in a welcoming gesture, and the movement of his damaged shoulder was as easy and natural as it had always been. Her mind almost filled in the missing limb as he stepped forward to embrace her, though his expression remained serious. "Good to see you, Sophie. I'm glad you came."

Once again, Sophie was rigid. One hand came up to pat Alika's back as he continued to hold her lightly but firmly, not crushing her close or taking any further liberties.

"I'm so sorry, Alika," she said against his shirt. "I should have visited you in the hospital. I should have been there for you."

He shook his head. "It is what it is."

Sophie gradually relaxed. Her face was pressed against the shoulder of his mutilated arm.

Memories of the bomb's explosion swamped her. He'd looked so magnificent standing in the doorway of the elevator, that fateful box tucked against his side. She blinked away more tears. "I let you down."

"It's okay. I was bummed, but not surprised you didn't want to see me. I know you, girl, and I knew you'd feel bad." He let go and stepped back, gesturing towards an open seating area done in refined bent bamboo furniture covered in Hawaiian print fabric. "Come, have a seat. As you can see, I'm just fine. I appreciate your coming all this way, though, just to tell me that."

"That was the first, and most important thing I came to say. But there is something else." Sophie gazed around the gracious room with its huge window that showcased the magnificent mountainscape of Hanalei. "This place is so beautiful."

"Thanks. I have a good architect," he grinned.

They seated themselves. Esther reappeared from the kitchen, carrying a small lacquered tray with a couple of glasses of yellow juice resting on it. Ice cubes clinked gently in the glasses, and Sophie could smell the tangy-sweet scent of passion fruit as Esther set down the tray. "Made this lilikoi juice myself this morning."

Sophie picked up her glass and sipped to swallow the lump in her throat. "Thank you, Mrs. Ka`awai. It's delicious."

"Esther, please. And now I've got a few more chores to do around here."

"Thanks, Tutu." Alika gestured toward the tray with his stump. "I'm adjusting to doing a lot of things one-handed. Balancing a tray with full glasses on it is a little out of my current skill set, but I'll get there eventually."

Sophie had expected him to be at least a little bitter, but there was none of that in his expression or demeanor as he picked up his glass. Esther left the room, and he smiled at Sophie over the rim. "Tutu has elected herself to be my chief cook and bottle washer. Who am I to argue, when she does it so well?"

"Men. You all just like to be taken care of," Sophie said, a ghost of a smile tugging at her own lips. She looked away, out the window of the great room. "I love your home."

"Thanks. Let me show you what I did with the koa wood I picked up on the Big Island when we saw each other last." He stood up. "It's in the kitchen."

Sophie followed Alika into the open, modern space with its granite counters, steel sinks, and wraparound windows. A banquette filled one corner, and the wood of that table gleamed with the unique iridescence of native Hawaiian hardwood. "I love it."

"I had cabinets made, too." He gestured to the storage areas above a large, shining range. "There was just enough wood for three kitchens like this."

Sophie admired the sleek design with its small brass canoes as hardware. "Really unique. It's hard to believe this came from those logs I saw in the back of your truck."

"There were many steps between the logs and what you see here. But I have a good crew."

Sophie wiped her hands on her skirt again, realizing as she did so that, though she was nervous about her news, the feelings she'd had for Alika, prior to the bomb attack, were gone. Any romantic interest she'd had in him must have been quenched by the guilt and worry she'd been carrying—and by her deepening involvement with Jake. Somehow that realization made it easier to face Alika head-on and look directly into his warm brown eyes.

"I came to see you, to apologize for how I acted when you were injured. But also, to tell you that I'm pregnant."

Alika's brows flew up and his eyes widened. "What?"

"Yes. We…didn't use anything that night. There's a chance…"

"I wondered, afterward…"

They both stared at the parquet squares of the kitchen floor.

"I'm seven or eight weeks along, I think." Sophie twisted her fingers together. "Will you take a paternity test? With Jake? So we can determine who the father is."

Alika looked away and his throat worked. "I figured you had moved on. I have too. For all our sakes, I hope this isn't my child."

Sophie swallowed, surprised at how much his words hurt even though she understood perfectly what he meant. "You don't have to do anything, regardless. I'm not asking you to take the test because I'm looking for help or support."

Alika turned back and his eyes blazed. "You think I'd abandon my responsibility to my own flesh and blood—my *ohana*? I thought you knew me."

Sophie wound her fingers together even tighter. "I meant no insult."

They stared at each other in tense silence.

Alika looked out the window and gave a deep sigh. "Of course, I'll take the test. And we'll all deal with whatever the results are."

"I don't expect you to understand, but I am happy I am pregnant. I thought I could never be a mother." She blinked stinging eyes.

Alika reached out and caught one of her hands. "Don't leave like this. We can be friends, at least. We were friends for years, and we might be parenting together."

"We don't know that," Sophie argued. "And I don't know where to go from here, in a manner of speaking."

"Me neither. But let me start by showing you around the whole house. I've got an idea where you and the baby could stay, when you visit."

"You're extrapolating excessively," Sophie protested, but let herself be led toward a wide staircase ascending to a second floor.

"I hope you'll plan on visiting, regardless." Alika squeezed her hand as they climbed the stairs. "In fact, I'd like to count on it. Just know you'll always have a soft spot to land if you need it. No matter what."

"Thanks," Sophie murmured. As awkward as the situation was, she felt better for his words, and for resolving so much so quickly. "I appreciate that."

CHAPTER TWENTY-SEVEN

SEATED in the office area on the jet, Connor ended the call from Felicia, frowning down at his phone. Jake had been shot? Who could be trying to take out one of his best operatives from a sniper position? The situation reminded him too much of Sophie's recent case when a contract killer had been after her.

The shooter had to be Akane Chang. Chang had no love for either Jake or Sophie.

Connor looked back down at his phone and scrolled to the text he had received from Sophie declining his help in getting to Kaua'i. *Good.* She'd be safe there, out of the way of this latest threat.

He should probably go check on Jake, but the man was likely out of commission for a while. The Ghost's time would be best spent trying to track the shooter, and all he needed was a computer for that.

Connor sat down and fired up his laptop. He hacked into a grid of surveillance cameras around the office building for Security Solutions in downtown Hilo. None of the feeds covered the particular area in which Jake's shooting had taken place, but by scrolling through one of the traffic camera backups, he was able to spot a man exiting the building across the street in the appropriate time frame.

The subject was close to six feet tall, wearing bulky, nondescript sweats, and carried a rifle-sized duffel bag over one shoulder. He wore a University of Hawaii Warriors ball cap, pulled low. His skin was medium dark in the black-and-white video.

The suspect got into a black Toyota 4Runner SUV parked on the corner. Connor paused the feed and magnified the license plate number.

Another quick hack, and he was into the Hawaii State vehicle registration site. He ran the number and came up with a car reported stolen of a completely different make. The plates had been changed.

This was Jake's shooter, for sure, but Connor had no useful information to pass on to authorities except that the man was roughly the same dimensions and race as Akane Chang, and was smart enough to have swapped the plates on what was likely a stolen vehicle.

Connor paced around, frustrated and worried. He missed his home in Thailand: the long, empty beaches of his island, Phi Ni, on which to run. He missed the company of his dog, Anubis, and the help and presence of his houseman, Nam. His home truly was his castle, and this enclosed container, parked on the hot tarmac of the Hilo airport, was far from ideal. Connor got up and went to the gym area that was a part of his office on the jet. He went through a routine on the Bowflex machine for a vigorous twenty minutes, getting blood flowing to his brain and extremities.

He was stalled on dealing with the shooter, but was sure it was Akane beginning the revenge spree that the man had sworn to complete in the courtroom a few short weeks ago.

The Ghost did have one unconventional weapon in his battle against the serial killer.

Done with his brief workout, Connor thumbed through his phone contacts. He sent Pim Wat a text that Akane was in Hilo and looking to make another attempt on Sophie's life via the Security Solutions office building.

It couldn't hurt to give her mother intel that was in their mutual interest—keep his pet assassin on alert and ready to move. He was doing his best to engineer a showdown between Akane and Pim Wat;

such killings were the Ghost's trademark, and they took careful engineering.

Connor smiled at the likelihood that the two would cancel each other out when they finally met. He'd spent hours imagining and orchestrating variations on that scenario. And if only one of them was the victor? That too was acceptable. Only one of his and Sophie's enemies would then remain alive to deal with, fifty percent less hassle.

Because whatever else she was, Pim Wat was also their enemy.

He slid his phone into his pocket and poured a glass of filtered water, drinking it at the sink, mentally probing for weaknesses in his plans.

As soon as Sophie heard that Jake was injured, she'd want to come back to Hilo to take care of him.

Connor had to keep Sophie out of danger until Akane, and hopefully Pim Wat, were dealt with.

He speed dialed another number. "Thom, can you return to the jet? I need to go to Kaua`i, ASAP."

CONNOR STOOD at the foot of the stairs of the jet, the waning light of evening slanting across the tarmac of the Lihue Airport on Kaua`i, as Sophie strode toward him. He admired the feline power of her stride contrasting with the feminine, fluttery skirt of her Mary Watson dress.

Sophie was frowning when she reached him, all but vibrating with distress, but she allowed Connor to embrace her in a brief hug. "Thanks so much for coming to fetch me. I can't believe someone shot Jake! I have to get back and see how he is doing."

"About that." Instead of ascending the jet's stairs, Connor turned her back toward the terminal. "We aren't going to the Big Island. I want you to stay here on Kaua`i for a few days. I've reserved a room for you at a very nice condo in Kalapaki Beach under your Mary Watson identity."

Sophie dug in her heels. "What? No. Jake needs me!"

"He does not. He's a big boy." Connor gritted his teeth, but made an effort to speak persuasively. "Felicia's looking after him, and it's just a flesh wound to his calf. Way more worrisome is that we both think the shooter was Akane, and he wants to kill you even more than he wants Jake."

"You don't understand. I have to get back to him." Sophie brushed past Connor and stomped up the stairs into the jet as if she could order Thom to take her back to the Big Island without him. Connor shook his head, following her up into the plane.

Sure enough, Sophie was arguing with his pilot, hands on her hips, voice raised. "We need to get back to the Big Island, Thom. It's urgent."

"I'm sorry, Sophie, that's not the flight plan Mr. Hamilton has filed." Thom Tang was a brave man, but today the Thai pilot looked a little terrified as he turned to Connor in blatant relief and appeal. "Here's Mr. Hamilton now. He can tell you." Thom scuttled into the cockpit and they both heard the distinct sound of the cockpit door locking.

"Sophie. Listen." Connor reached for her arm.

She shook him off. "No. I'm not going to listen. My boyfriend has been shot. I'm going back to Hilo to see if he is all right."

"Jake's fine. He's had stitches, and his leg is in a support boot. He's at home resting. I just had a call from Felicia. She even got him settled in bed in his apartment and took the dogs out for a walk. He's passed out from pain meds and will be feeling a lot better in the morning. You can talk to him then."

Their gazes clashed.

Connor took off his Sheldon Hamilton glasses and set them aside. He grasped Sophie's shoulders. "Jake would not want you running back into the line of fire. Let this situation play out. Let

Akane show himself, so we can catch him and deal with him. Then you can play Florence Nightingale to Jake all you want."

"Florence Nightingale?" A frown-wrinkle appeared between her elegant brows.

Connor wished he could smooth that line with his thumb, maybe put his lips right there. He squeezed her shoulders instead. "Famous war nurse. Braver and stronger than an army. Which both Jake and I know you are. But trust me on this—he wouldn't want you anywhere that put you in danger. And don't forget—you've got someone else to keep safe now, too."

Sophie's hand dropped to her slim waist. Her whole body sagged. "This doesn't feel right. Jake will think I don't care, that I'm staying with Alika."

"You can call Jake tomorrow and set him straight. Tell him your boss is making an executive decision, and Hamilton's a real bastard. Which we both know is true."

Sophie looked up swiftly. Connor smiled.

She smiled back. "You *are* a bastard. But at least you're...*my* bastard." Sophie turned away as heat flushed Connor's chest and neck at her words. "All right. We can stay here, just for tonight. I'll leave Jake a message, though, and talk to him tomorrow. I need to make sure he knows I want to be with him." She took out her phone and strode into Connor's office, shutting the door.

Connor's office was the one part of the plane where he didn't run surveillance devices, and Sophie knew that.

"Damn it." Connor shook his head ruefully. *He'd give his left nut to know what Sophie was saying on that message to Jake.*

But another part of him sure as hell didn't want to hear her declarations of love for another man.

Connor still had no idea how the talk with Alika had gone, though from Sophie's demeanor it didn't seem like the possible pregnancy had thrown them into each other's arms.

Sophie re-emerged from the office. Pink spots burned high on her cheekbones and her honey-brown eyes flashed. "Felicia answered Jake's phone before I could leave a message. She assured me Jake is in good hands and being cared for." She picked up the backpack she'd dropped near the door of the jet. "Where is this condo? Let's go."

Connor wasn't about to argue with her change of heart. He followed Sophie down the steps. Clearly, something was amiss between Sophie and Jake, and the addition of Felicia was complicating things—but that wasn't a situation he had any intention of helping resolve.

He was a bastard, indeed. But he was *her* bastard.

CHAPTER TWENTY-EIGHT

Day Six

Sophie stood on the deck of her little condo, looking out at the idyllic setting of Kalapaki Beach on the south side of Kaua'i. The sun was up at last, gilding nearby palm trees with golden light. The wind, usually such a part of life on that side of the island, hadn't come up yet, and little peeling waves were being ridden directly in front of the resort by longboard surfers, standup paddlers, and body-boarders.

Sophie stroked her phone with the ball of her thumb, gazing at the vista. *Was it too early to try to call Jake?*

"This is Felicia." Sophie had been shocked when their receptionist had answered Jake's phone when she'd tried to call him on his cell from Connor's office the day before.

Sophie's voice was sharp. "What are you doing with Jake's phone?"

"I took his phone to monitor it, while he's sleeping from the pain meds. I thought it would be helpful if I could answer questions from family members or the cops, if they called." Felicia sounded clear and confident.

Of course. That made sense.

Sophie felt bad about the possessive, suspicious feeling growing in her chest. Felicia was just doing her job, looking out for them both. "I'm so glad you're there to take care of him. How's he doing?"

"He has a four-inch-long, two-inch-deep gouge in the back of his calf, and he's lucky to be alive. I guess he dropped something on the sidewalk and bent to retrieve it, or the sniper would have nailed him."

"Evil spawn of the devil!" Sophie swore. She pressed her hand over her thumping heart, imagining getting the news that Jake was so unexpectedly dead.

"What's that?"

"Sorry. I curse in my native language. That sounds like a serious wound."

"I imagine it hurts like crazy. He had stitches and he's on antibiotics and has some good drugs for pain, so it's just a matter of time until he's back on his feet."

"I'm here on Kaua'i on personal business, as I texted you. Mr. Hamilton flew over and we've been discussing the situation. I'm glad the injury wasn't too serious." *What an understatement.* "Can you tell me more details about what happened?"

"Sure. From what I gathered, Jake left our building, and somebody shot at him from an apartment across the street. He took cover behind a car. The shooter tried again and blew the window out on the car. Jake, being Jake, decided to go after the guy. Never mind that he was bleeding like a stuck pig." Felicia's voice wobbled. "Jake figured out where the shot came from, went across the street and found the room. Unfortunately, or fortunately, depending on how you look at it, the shooter was gone by the time he got there. He directed the police to the location, and they ran prints on a bottle that was left behind. They identified Akane Chang as the shooter."

Sophie swallowed and sat down abruptly in Connor's office

chair. "That man won't have the decency to die, or at least stay in jail. *Foul slime!*"

"Your foreign swearing sounds so cool, better than me just yelling, 'that evil asshole!'" Felicia said. "I gather Chang's quite the public enemy number one."

"And he has sworn revenge on Jake and me for testifying against him. Did the police send any support to guard Jake?"

"I've been trying to get a police officer stationed outside Jake's room, but they're acting like I'm a hysterical girlfriend or something. It's super frustrating," Felicia said angrily.

"And it doesn't help when his actual girlfriend is on another island," Sophie said. "Our CEO, Mr. Hamilton, is insisting that I stay here on Kaua'i until the Chang threat is neutralized. I'll call Jake in the morning, but can you make sure he knows that I'm very concerned, and on my way back as soon as possible?"

"I sure will. Don't worry. I'm taking good care of him, and your dogs, too." Felicia had said goodbye and hung up.

Yes, every word of that conversation with Felicia yesterday felt chiseled into Sophie's brain. She wished she didn't feel jealous, territorial, and possessive just thinking of Felicia helping Jake into bed, fixing food for him, and taking their dogs for a walk. It was stupid and wrong and beneath her.

She understood Jake's difficulty with her relationship with Alika now.

This was good. Educational. Painful as hell.

Sophie turned away from the ocean view at the sound of the knocker at her door. *Probably Connor, with some new update or plan.*

Room service had arrived, a breakfast for two. Sophie accepted the cart and peeked under metal lids covering a delicious-looking breakfast of eggs, waffles, bacon, and fruit. She checked in with her stomach. This morning it rumbled with hunger, not morning sickness. This might be one of the mornings she was going to be able to eat.

The knocker sounded again, and Sophie let Connor in. "Thanks for thinking of breakfast. I'm actually hungry today."

"Excellent."

They sat on the balcony overlooking the ocean. Sophie liked that he wasn't wearing his dark contacts or glasses—he knew she hated his Sheldon Hamilton disguise, and he'd come over only wearing sunglasses that he could put on if anyone saw them.

"I feel guilty being here, having such a nice meal in this setting." Sophie fiddled with her napkin as Connor served fruit onto her plate.

"Guilt is a waste of time and energy." Connor poured pink guava juice into her glass. Sophie inhaled deeply before she sipped, enjoying the sweet, tangy smell of it, as he went on. "Guilt doesn't help the person you feel guilty about, either. It just steals any joy you might have had in the moment. A useless emotion."

"I shouldn't be talking to you about my relationships, but I... don't know what to do."

"Yeah, you probably shouldn't. But tell me anyway." Connor poured coffee into his mug from a carafe.

Sophie shut her eyes to enjoy the cool, unique flavor of the guava juice. "I was going to call Jake. But I'm worried that Felicia will answer. Worried what it will mean if she does."

Connor laughed. "You're afraid of your receptionist?"

"Don't underestimate that young woman. Felicia's a psychology graduate student. She's just doing office temp work while she completes a doctorate in clinical psychology." Sophie took a bite of her eggs, relieved not to feel nausea when she did so. "Felicia's smart and hard-working, and really admires Jake. She is very careful with me, but I get the feeling she wouldn't be sad if we broke up. She's very appropriate in her communications, but I don't want to have to talk to her about Jake again."

"You're not even going to try to call him?" Connor reached over and grabbed her phone. "Coward. Let me do it then."

The phone was already unlocked. Connor scrolled to Jake's

number in Sophie's favorites, and pressed it. Sophie frowned, but allowed him to. She *was* a coward.

Connor lifted a brow at her as he removed the cover from his plate and picked up his fork, the phone set on speaker between them. He took several bites of eggs while it rang.

Jake's voice came on. "Sophie?" He sounded rough, his voice scratchy.

"Hey, Jake. This is Hamilton. I'm here with Sophie on Kaua'i. We thought we'd get in touch and see how you're doing." Connor's tone was upbeat and businesslike.

"What are you doing on Kaua'i?" Sophie could hear Jake's confusion, and she reached for the phone and took it off speaker.

"Jake. Are you all right? I was so worried. By the way, I just took you off speaker."

"I'm fine. Just a flesh wound. What are you doing with Hamilton over there?" She could hear the rasp of his whiskers as he rubbed his face, the sound of his yawn.

"Hamilton thinks that, since the shooter was Akane Chang, I should stay here. Where it's safe, supposedly."

"He's right. Hopefully, the cops get Akane soon." A pause. "What did Alika say about the paternity test?"

"Alika agreed to it." A silence stretched out. Sophie rubbed the scar on her cheekbone. He clearly wanted to know more about Alika's response to the news, but right in front of Connor wasn't the place or time—although Connor appeared oblivious, shoveling in his breakfast, Sophie knew better. She rushed on. "Felicia said she took care of you yesterday. And the dogs."

"She sure did. The dogs are fine, keeping me company. She said she'd be back at lunchtime to walk them. Don't worry about me, Sophie. It's just a gash, as I'm sure Felicia told you. I'll be back on my feet in a few days, on crutches."

"Give me back the phone," Connor said. "I have some news for him."

Sophie handed the phone over.

"Jake, it's Hamilton again and I'm putting you back on speaker. I've arranged for a couple of our security guys from Oahu to come look after you. I've also put in a call to the FBI about this attack by an escaped felon on one of my operatives. I'm putting pressure on the FBI about my team's safety, and letting them know that Hilo PD has a positive ID on Akane as the shooter, in case the officers didn't report it right away. I hope you don't mind if I keep your girlfriend here for a while, out of the line of fire."

"Thanks. Yes. Keep her there; I'll sleep better knowing she's safe." The gratitude in Jake's voice brought tears to Sophie's eyes; she blinked hard.

"I'll set Sophie up to work on the Merrie Monarch and other cases over here. Once the cops get a line on Akane, I'll return her to you." Connor looked down and away; Sophie couldn't read his expression.

"Thanks. Especially for the security guys, since Hilo PD doesn't seem to have the staffing to give me any coverage, and I'm a sitting duck for Akane laid up like this. We rented the apartments under our aliases, but that's not much protection if he's got us under surveillance. Felicia is doing a great job keeping everything going, but I don't know how good she'd be guarding my door with a gun. Thanks for making sure Sophie is safe. If I know her, she's not making it easy."

Connor met Sophie's gaze with a blue-green one. "You have no idea."

Sophie leaned closer to the microphone on the phone. "I will see you soon, Jake. Feel better. I miss you." She ended the call.

CHAPTER TWENTY-NINE

Day Seventeen

THE BEAUTIFUL VIEW of Kalapaki Beach had begun to fade in novelty eleven days later. Sophie paced in front of the sliding glass window restlessly, on the phone with an obstetrician's office on the Big Island. She had been using the enforced downtime to address various neglected areas of her life, beginning with interviewing doctors that she hoped might be a fit for her prenatal care. So far, she hadn't decided if she wanted to try a natural birth with a midwife or go the more traditional hospital route.

Not having a partner to talk it over with was a lack Sophie felt keenly. She'd been calling Marcella to hash things over as much as she could, but between the FBI's busy schedule and not knowing anything about the topic, her friend had not been much help. Her other friend, Lei, had recently lost a pregnancy. Sophie was reluctant to poke at that wound with her many questions, so had held back from contacting her.

She and Alika had both submitted blood to the Oahu clinic doing the paternity test, and Jake had mailed in his sample. They were all just waiting for the processing. Every morning Sophie held her breath as she checked her email.

If she just knew who the baby's father was, she could talk to *him* about all of this.

But the only person she really had available was Connor.

Connor had been endlessly helpful, researching questions that Sophie had, running statistical analysis on best health practices for her to try, fetching her treats and providing ideas to alleviate her nausea, and giving her work to keep her busy.

Work was the best thing she could find to keep her mind off the situation. Sophie did as much as she could on the Merrie Monarch case, wrapping up her notes for Kim Kauwa and the Tourism Authority. She called Esther and had a three-way conference call with both women, letting them know unequivocally that everything pointed to Penny Chang as the festival funds embezzler. She had a follow-up phone therapy session with Dr. Wilson and continued to sort through her feelings about being a mother.

She'd called Jake several times, but their conversations were stilted, focused on the practicalities of the dogs and the office. The question of the baby's paternity loomed large. Avoidance seemed better to Sophie; perhaps she and Jake could work things out only in person. Jake must have concluded the same, because he didn't call her either.

Alika had invited her to dinner one night at his home, and Sophie met a host of his lovely Hawaiian relatives. However, she sensed his reserve, the strain of waiting to know the results of the test inhibiting their friendship. Once again, avoidance seemed best.

And now, she was more than ready to leave Kaua`i.

Room service breakfast arrived, as usual, but this time Connor was the one to roll the cart into her room. "Surprise. I headed the guy off in the hall."

Sophie faced him, dressed for travel. She pointed to her packed bag, lying on the bed. "It's time to go back to the Big Island. Chang has not surfaced. I can't live indefinitely in this condo. I need to get back to my apartment, my dog, and my boyfriend. In addition, I've got an appointment with an obstetrician this afternoon in Hilo. You can take me, or I'll go by myself."

Connor cocked his head to the side. "You've certainly built up a head of steam. Were you thinking I was going to try to dissuade you? I was actually going to propose that we head back today, as well. Thom already has the flight plan submitted. We'll have to work on a trap for Akane Chang, since he hasn't shown himself. Now, can we take time to eat breakfast before we get going?"

Sophie spontaneously threw her arms around Connor. "Thank you! You've been my best friend through all of this. I don't know what I would've done without you."

She thought she might have felt his lips against her neck. "Anything for you, Sophie." His whispered words did not make Sophie uncomfortable—he meant them. He had demonstrated the truth of them over and over, in large ways and small; and it was gradually healing the wound of his betrayal.

SOPHIE'S APARTMENT in Hilo smelled stale and musty as she opened the door. After the bright colors and luxurious surroundings of the condo on Kaua`i, the bare little place seemed dark and drab. Glancing around the barely furnished rooms, Sophie realized that she hadn't felt depressed the entire time she'd been on Kaua`i.

In fact, she hadn't had an episode since she found out she was pregnant.

Maybe something was different with her hormones. Maybe knowing that she had this new, important purpose, despite its many challenges, had changed something.

Ginger nudged Sophie's dangling hand with her head. Tank, on the other side of her, jostled forward into the apartment. Sophie let go of the dogs' leashes, and they bounded inside to re-explore this familiar den.

Sophie had arrived on the Big Island only an hour before. She'd said goodbye to Connor at the airport; he'd been continuing on to Oahu to meet with Bix on Security Solutions business.

Sophie was more than ready to resume her life, even filled with all the nerve-wracking changes on the horizon, beginning with reuniting with Jake. She had gone straight to Jake's apartment, only to find it empty.

She'd texted him: *"I'm at your place. Hamilton finally gave the OK on returning. Looking forward to seeing you! Where are you?"*

"The office. Up to my eyebrows with a new client. The dogs would welcome an outing."

Nothing about seeing her. Nothing personal...

Sophie's belly hollowed with distress—or possible morning sickness, which was still hitting her at random times throughout the day. She took out a strong ginger candy that Connor had bought her for nausea, and sucked on it.

She didn't have time to mope over Jake and his lack of enthusiasm about getting together. She had to drop her things, take the dogs out, and head to the Big Island Birth Clinic.

CHAPTER THIRTY

JAKE CURSED as he set his phone face down on the desk. He just wasn't ready to deal with his relationship with Sophie without knowing the baby's paternity.

"What? Going potty mouth on me, old man?" Felicia called from the reception desk in the other room. Jake kept his office door open, and they yelled back and forth frequently.

Felicia had been a rock for Jake during the time Sophie had been gone. She'd driven him to his doctor's appointments, kept him fed, exercised the dogs, managed his security guys and all they needed, and joined him in the evenings for pizza, beer, and hilarious old movies like *Monty Python's Life of Brian* and *The Pink Panther* series.

Felicia had made the time he was healing and hiding from Akane Chang tolerable. He was going to miss their camaraderie. "Sophie's back. She has a doctor's appointment this afternoon, but she'll be in tomorrow."

"Terrific. I'll put that in the scheduler." Felicia was all business.

Jake refocused on the report in front of him with an effort. He was finishing up a bid to install a new AI security system out at that dot-commer's house in Hamakua. He'd had to oversee others doing all the prep due to his leg, but at least his injury had allowed him to drive out to the estate yesterday and check all the specs in person.

Jake heard the buzzer sound as the office door opened. They didn't get many drop-ins, but it wasn't unheard of, and the security guy at the door would have screened the visitor. Felicia's perky greeting came next: "Welcome to Security Solutions. How can we help you today?"

"I need to speak with Sophie Ang or Jake Dunn, please." A man's voice. *Jake knew that voice.*

"Do you have an appointment?" Felicia asked.

Jake stood up, grabbed his crutch, and hopped to the door of his office. "Terence Chang. This is a surprise."

The young local man looked haggard. Dark circles hung like hammocks beneath intelligent brown eyes. His hair was mussed, and rusty streaks marked his clothing. "I need help on an urgent matter."

Jake swung his door wide and gestured toward the chair in front of his desk. "Please, have a seat." Jake turned back to Felicia. "We're not to be disturbed. No calls, no interruptions."

He shut the door firmly on her open-mouthed expression.

Jake returned to sit behind his desk, leaning his crutch against the wall. "You're the last person I'd have expected as a client, Chang."

"I'm not a client yet. I'm not telling you anything about what's going on until you sign a nondisclosure agreement." Terence's hands were trembling. He kept his gaze on the floor between his feet. Chang was clearly in shock from a serious trauma.

"Got one right here. Our standard contract." Jake took a blank form out of his desk and slid it across to Terence, along with a pen. "But you should know that I don't have legal confidentiality protections like a lawyer, priest, or a psychologist does. I can be compelled to testify in court, so think hard about what you're going to tell me about those bloodstains on your clothing."

Terence looked down at himself, an expression of surprise lifting his brows. "Oh that. It's not mine."

"I didn't expect that it was." Jake stared at the other man levelly.

Terence signed the contract and pushed it back across the desk to Jake. "I didn't do it." He dropped his face into his hands. "I've done things—but not this thing."

Jake sat back, laced his fingers over his flat belly, and waited for the man to speak.

Terence leaned forward, his elbows on his knees, and pushed his hands through his normally immaculately barbered hair, disturbing it even further. "Akane's started killing everyone I love or care about, just like he said he would. I just came from my uncle Henry's place. There were pieces of him all over the house. This is his blood."

"Did you call the police?" Jake rapped out.

"Anonymously. From a pay phone. I know how the cops work. They've been gunning for me for a while now. I didn't touch anything but…I must have. I don't know how this blood got on me." Terence looked up at Jake with red-rimmed eyes. "Akane called me and left a message to go check on Uncle; I feared the worst, but it was worse than I'd even imagined. He's checking off his list, and my uncle was the closest thing I had to a father. My own dad was killed when I was a baby."

"He already tried to get me, as I'm sure you're aware." Jake extended his bandaged leg, still clad in the support boot. "Tell me something I don't know, like where that psycho can be found. Our whole firm has been searching for him. The FBI is looking for him, and the Big Island cops are looking for him. And still no one knows where he is."

"Well, if I knew where he was, I wouldn't be here." Terence dropped his face into his hands. "You've got to help me find him, before he gets Julie."

"Julie Weathersby?" Jake's voice sharpened.

"Julie Weathersby, yes." Terence looked down at his hands. "She is…special to me. I warned her parents to take her out of the country, and they have. I don't know where, and I don't want to know. In case Akane tries to torture her location out of me."

Julie had been the object of a missing persons case that Jake and

Sophie had wrapped up recently. Terence had rescued the girl from Akane Chang. Her story that she had been rescued by Terence and that they'd fallen in love had sounded like a fairy tale cooked up by a girl with Stockholm Syndrome, but looking at Terence's tormented expression, Jake reconsidered.

"Geez, Terence, dramatic much?" Jake forced a laugh. "We'll get this guy. We have ways the cops don't. What I need from you is a complete family tree of the Changs, with names, addresses, and locations—and a list of all of the allies that you can think of, and any info regarding landholdings, businesses, et cetera, that could help our agency find him."

"I figured you'd need that. My cousin is on her way."

Jake's office door opened. "Terence. Mr. Dunn." A young woman with a regal bearing stood in the doorway.

"I told this woman she couldn't just barge in," Felicia hollered from the reception area. "But she did anyway!"

"This is my cousin Emma," Terence said. "Em, thanks for coming and bringing what I asked you to."

Jake could see a resemblance to Terence in the woman's tilted brown eyes and full, determined mouth. Emma wore jeans and a bright purple shirt emblazoned with *Badass Bitch* in glittery writing. Her arms jangled with gold bracelets, and she wore a pistol strapped to her hip.

"Don't know why we need these stupid *haole* rent-a-cops," Emma growled in Terence's direction. "We can handle this."

"You didn't see what he did to my uncle," Terence said.

"Even so. But it's your dime, cuz." Emma stomped across the room and slapped down a small external storage device in front of Jake. "Terence, he da boss. He say come, bring you this, I bring you this."

"What is it?" Jake held up the drive.

"A complete list of all of the Chang family and their closest associates. Those who might be aligned with Akane are marked with an asterisk." Emma put her hands on her rounded hips. Her dark eyes flicked over Jake contemptuously. "This better not get out of your hands, or I know where to find you."

"It won't. We'll give you and your cousin the same top-quality service we give all of our clients," Jake said. "Why don't you have a seat?"

"No. I have a memorial service to plan for Terence's uncle." Emma sailed back out of the office and slammed the door.

"She's a bit of a hothead, my cuz," Terence said. "But she kicks ass."

"I have no doubt." Jake waggled the drive in Terence's direction. "Lucky for you, Sophie, who's our computer expert, just got back on island. She'll be able to hunt for more detail online with this info. It might give us an idea of who's hiding him, where, because he must have help."

"No doubt." To judge by his scowl, Terence seemed to be waging an internal debate. Finally, he said, "What do you think about using Sophie for bait? To lure Akane out into the open?"

"Screw that. Let's use *you* as bait, Terence," Jake flared. "You're the one he really wants."

Terence's eyes widened. "How did you know?" he whispered.

CHAPTER THIRTY-ONE

HOW HAD THIS MUSCLEHEAD, Jake Dunn, guessed that Akane wanted Terence most of all? As far as Terence had been able to discern, no one was talking about the massacre of Akane's family.

Terence looked down at his hands, turning them over. He must have touched some part of Uncle's body, because dried blood made dark lines in the folds of his fingers.

And it was on his clothes. He'd wiped his hands on his shirt at some point.

He had no memory of any of that.

What Akane had done to Uncle had been too terrible even to process, but bits of memory blasted his brain randomly with images he could never unsee: Uncle's chopped off, curled-up hands, one on either side of a plate set on the dining room table. His torso, spilling entrails on the kitchen floor. His legs, propped as if sitting, on a chair.

Akane's version of humor.

The next stop for Terence, after this, was his lawyer's office.

Terence looked up at the Security Solutions agent at last.

Jake Dunn was staring back at him from smoke-colored eyes, his chair tilted back, his fingers laced over his belly. He looked hard, dangerous, like a damn good poker player.

Maybe the guy wasn't as dumb as he'd assumed.

"You can tell me the real reason you're here any time now," Dunn said. "Or not. Makes no never mind to me. You signed a contract, and we're on the clock. It's running on your dime now, as your cousin said."

"All right. I'll tell you what I can. I'm in the middle of a war with Akane for control of Chang Enterprises." Terence sat back and imitated Dunn's pose. "It's important that I win. For everyone's good."

"Ah. You're taking over the family for the good of all." Dunn's tone dripped sarcasm. "I'm looking at the next Big Island mafia boss right now. Don't know what you need Security Solutions for."

"It's a civil war, and I need manpower." Terence kept his temper in check with difficulty. "I was groomed to take my grandmother Healani Chang's place as head of the family when she passed. But I didn't want it. I wanted to go legit, so I built my own business online. My cousin Byron stepped up, and while he lacked vision, he was a solid leader. Things were stable. Then the situation with Akane exploded. You and Ang were at the heart of that." Terence needed to move. He stood up and paced. "Akane has supporters in the family, people who mistake his brutality for strength. And he was building alliances behind Byron's back. Then Byron was murdered. I wouldn't be surprised if Akane was behind it." Terence turned to meet Dunn's gaze. "I realized I was the only one smart enough, strong enough, with enough resources, to keep Akane from taking over. So, I made my move." He pushed a hand through his rumpled hair. "Now he's back, and it's a hostile situation. It will either be him or me running the family business, and trust me—it should not be him."

"I agree with you there. And thanks for being straight up. What do you need from us? Manpower we've got. Investigative strength we've got. Even great home security systems, we've got."

"I know all about your AI nanny cam security system. That might be nice later. Right now, I need your best-trained security operatives. I hired some mercs from the Mainland who are keeping my house and Emma safe, but I need more. We might also need to go on the offensive with some of my relatives after Akane is caught. But catching Akane is my number one priority. I don't want one more person I care about to be hurt."

"Like Julie Weathersby?" Dunn tilted his head. "I thought she was just a Stockholm nutcase when she was going on and on about you, and how you two fell in love."

Heat flushed Terence's face. "She…talked about me to you?" He hadn't seen Julie since the day she left to return to her parents, and he'd missed her every moment since.

"Oh yeah. When Sophie and I interviewed her about what happened with Akane, she couldn't say enough about how great you were. We thought she was a little loco, just hero worshipping her rescuer." Dunn shrugged. "But now I'm guessing it was mutual."

"Doesn't matter. That chapter's over, but I must do all I can to protect her. I'd appreciate anything you can put together." Terence clenched his fists. "I need help to win this war."

"Well, I for one like the idea of using you as bait," Dunn said. "I think we could build a solid plan around that. Not even joking. Sophie texted me that she'll be in the office tomorrow. We'll work something up. In the meantime, I'll contact our corporate head on Oahu, and see how many security personnel they can send over. I didn't see you come in with anyone—got a security detail on you?"

"No. I don't want to seem weak to my relatives. The men I hired are keeping an eye on my house and business."

"At this point, you're going to seem dead if you don't have a bodyguard at all times," Dunn said briskly. He tapped his computer screen and spoke into a voice intercom there. "Felicia, how many security specialists do we have on tap, here on the Big Island?"

"That would be none, Jake. You and Sophie are the personnel

here," the girl said, her voice piped through the computer speakers. "Not including your own two security staff."

Dunn grimaced at Terence. "You're not the only startup around here, Chang. But we will get you covered. Why don't we meet tomorrow morning and hash out the details? We can come out to your place if you prefer."

"No, here is fine." Terence extended a hand. "Thanks for the help."

"We want your psycho cousin as much as you do." Dunn's eyes were the color of a steel blade.

CHAPTER THIRTY-TWO

Sophie had meant to stay up and awake to talk to Jake when he got home from work. She'd decided to nap just a little, but the next time she woke, it was to the cool sensation of a night breeze passing over her body, and Tank's deep growl.

Sophie sat up on the futon bed, blinking in alarm. Connor had said he was sending over more security personnel from Oahu, but they hadn't arrived yet—or had they?

Moonlight backlit the shape of a woman standing just outside the screen door on her deck. *Was it Pim Wat?* Possibly, but Sophie didn't recognize her mother's outline.

She couldn't see a weapon in the woman's open hands, loose at her sides. There was nothing overtly threatening in her stance, but Tank's growl increased in volume, and Ginger, curled up against Sophie's back on the bed, raised her head, her chest rumbling with her own growl. The two were about to break into full-blown barking. Sophie put a hand on each dog's ruff and quieted them.

"You'd better tell me who you are and what you are doing here." Sophie turned on the floor lamp beside her bed as the woman stepped forward.

Light fell on a golden-skinned, triangular face with close-set dark eyes and a mouth that had never seen orthodontia. Dark hair was pulled back in a braid that brushed the tops of her hips. The woman wore a long-sleeved tee, yoga pants, and felt-bottomed slip-on shoes, all in black.

An instant feeling of recognition resonated in Sophie.

"Sophie Malee. It is I, Armita." The woman spoke in Thai. "Your nanny from long ago."

Armita was tiny, even shorter than Pim Wat, and so slender she seemed almost cartoonlike, a stick drawing of a woman, her head larger than her body.

Sophie tossed her blanket aside and sat up. She was still fully dressed, never having planned to pass out for the night like she had. Her abrupt movement made the dogs lunge to their feet and give in to the barking she'd barely restrained.

Sophie shooed them back, shushing them, and slid the screen door open. "I remember you, Armita. Please come in." A maelstrom of emotions roiled in her chest; the last time she had seen Armita, the woman had been bleeding and unconscious on the floor of Sophie's bedroom when Sophie was kidnapped at the age of seven.

Armita slipped past Sophie and extended her hands to the dogs to sniff. Both whimpered and whuffed with excitement at having a visitor, their tails wagging as they crowded against her.

There was nowhere to sit in the bare apartment, so Sophie perched on the bed's edge, observing Armita as the Thai woman caressed the dogs while she looked around the space, and then sat beside Sophie. The dogs calmed, but cuddled close, leaning against her legs. Their instant bond with her former nanny relaxed Sophie further.

"I had to speak with you," Armita said. "But you must not tell her I came."

"Tell who? I'm still in shock to see you after all these years," Sophie said.

"You must not tell Pim Wat that I spoke with you. Or I will get much, much trouble." Armita grasped Sophie's hands; hers felt small and soft as a child's. Her eyes welled as she scanned Sophie's face searchingly. "Your scar. It's not as bad as I worried it would be. You are still so beautiful."

Sophie was unsure what to ask first—she had so many questions. "Why did you come here in the middle of the night? And climb up to my room?" She gestured to the deck. "It's three stories to the ground. I didn't think anyone could approach that way."

"You must not tell Pim Wat I came," Armita repeated. Her mouth quivered. "Please."

"All right, I won't. Did Mother fire you or something, after the kidnapping?" Sophie squeezed Armita's hands reassuringly, disturbed that the woman was so agitated and fearful. "She told me that you left—that you quit working for us because you didn't want a job where you were put in danger." Now Sophie's chin wobbled as she remembered how devastated she'd been—Armita had been her mother in everything but name from her earliest memories. The nanny's abrupt disappearance, on top of Sophie's trauma from the kidnapping, had always haunted her. "Where did you go?"

"I was not fired. I am Pim Wat's personal servant; I have been all of these years. She would not let me see you after I had failed in my duty to protect you." She let go of Sophie's hands and turned away, her slender shoulders slumping. "I am so ashamed."

"What? Two armed men broke in and took me! They hit you on the head!" Sophie exclaimed. Anger lit in her breast as she remembered sleepless nights in her little bed, crying for Armita—and the poor woman had been blamed, and kept away! "I can't believe this. Mother would not be so cruel."

Armita's eyes were hard as black diamonds as she gazed at Sophie. "You do not know your mother the way I do. She says she is cruel to make me strong. She said that you too must be strong."

"I was seven years old! I'd been kidnapped and kept in a closet for ten days!" Sophie shook her head. "But you did not answer my question. Why did you come to my apartment the way you did? Why now, after all these years?"

"I came when she wouldn't miss me. I came a way that would not be seen by those watching you. I came now because I had to warn you."

"Who is watching me? And warn me of what?"

Armita stood. "There are many watching you, and one of them wants you dead. But your mother—she wants you to serve her. She wants to own you, like she owns me. And she is planning something. She usually tells me everything, but she has not told me this, and it worries me." She drew a breath and sighed it out, her fingertips touching Sophie's arm lightly. "Do not go to Thailand, to the stronghold of the Yām Khûmkạn. You may not be able to leave if you do."

"I won't," Sophie said fiercely. "I'm pregnant, Armita. I must protect my baby." She hadn't meant to tell the woman, but the words had just popped out. *She still trusted Armita.*

Armita's face seemed to light with a glow of joy as she smiled. "Oh, Sophie Malee! How wonderful!" She leaned forward to embrace Sophie, her small hands fluttering around Sophie's face and hair like butterflies. "In my fondest dreams, we were reunited. And I cared for your children as if they were my own." Her eyes were wet. "I am so happy! I thought you could not have children, after Assan Ang."

It was jarring that she seemed to know everything about Sophie, but oddly reassuring too.

"I thought I could not have children either. This has been a surprise, and will be a big adjustment, but I'm happy about it. And I would love you to be my child's nanny. Leave my mother. Come live with me. I know I will need help; I can't do this alone."

Armita stepped back. Her smile was deeply sad. "If only that were possible. And now, we both have a secret to keep from Pim Wat. I must go."

"Please don't! Stay with me until the morning, and go out the front way," Sophie pleaded. She patted the bed. "There is plenty of room, and I will sleep better with you here, I know it."

Armita shook her head. Tears gleamed on her high cheekbones in the light from the lamp. "I am so glad to have seen you, and I will be watching out for you as best I can. Remember my warning." The petite woman slid open the door, climbed over the balcony railing, and disappeared.

CHAPTER THIRTY-THREE

BY THE TIME Sophie went out on the balcony and looked over the edge, Armita was gone. "She's a ninja," Sophie whispered. "Was that whole encounter even real?"

Sophie went back inside. The dogs milled around, sensing her agitation, and she wanted to go for a run—but nausea tickled the back of her throat at the mere thought.

Where was Jake? Why hadn't he come and let himself in and gotten into bed with her to snuggle, if nothing else? If she had needed confirmation that something was very wrong, she now had it.

Sophie went to the sink, filled a glass with water, and stared out at the night as she sipped, mulling the situation over.

Maybe she should just go to him. Let herself into his apartment and get in bed with him. They didn't have to talk. Their bodies had spoken best, anyway.

But did she want to be with him, when he might not want to be with her? His love for her wasn't very strong if he couldn't forgive her for being with Alika just one time, when she and Jake hadn't even been a couple…if this was a "deal breaker" for him, was he the right partner for her?

But if they were having a baby together, they would *have* to work things out.

And if they weren't, it was better to know now, and end the romantic aspect of their partnership. "Like ripping off a Band-Aid," Marcella's voice said in her mind.

"Ugh," Sophie said aloud. "Oh, it hurts." She wrapped her arms around herself tightly.

Sophie understood how Jake felt about Alika so much better now, understood his wound from the past and how it made it hard for him to imagine being a father to another man's child. Maybe he wasn't up to that challenge, but she owed it to him to reach out, for all the times he had reached out to her.

Resolved, Sophie pushed the dogs aside, locked them in her apartment, and exited onto the exterior corridor. Would she encounter Jake's security detail outside his door?

No one was there, to her surprise. Maybe they were watching from another observation point? Sophie glanced around but saw nothing untoward.

She'd been able to get into his apartment to retrieve the dogs, so she was surprised that, when she unlocked the door, a chain and bar were on inside.

Sophie slid her phone out of her pocket and called Jake's cell. It went to voicemail.

She would have to wake him up. How embarrassing. How vulnerable. And yet…

Sophie knocked, leaning into the crack in the door, calling gently inside. "Jake! Let me in. It's Sophie."

She heard quick, light footsteps and recoiled as Felicia's face, framed by tousled blonde hair, appeared in the narrow opening of the door. Sophie grasped the doorframe, feeling faint.

"Sophie! Jake looked in on you and said you were sleeping." Felicia whispered. She shut the door. Sophie listened to the chain and bar being disengaged. She opened the door again. "We didn't want to wake you."

"Are you and Jake...together?" Sophie whispered.

"Yes. No! I mean, we got done at work late. I brought some pizza over for you both, but you were in bed already, and so we watched a movie and..." The girl stammered, her cheeks pink. "I fell asleep. Jake's in bed, and he took some meds. His leg..."

"I understand," Sophie said woodenly. She stepped back from the door. "It's fine. He knows where to find me if he would like to talk."

Sophie turned and fled.

She reentered her apartment, her heart pounding, her mouth dry. *Felicia and Jake!*

Her mind couldn't seem to stop playing awful pictures of the two in bed together. Whether or not Felicia was telling the truth, the fact that Jake had chosen Felicia's company over her own was a statement.

On top of the bizarre and disturbing visit from Armita, trying to go back to sleep after this upset seemed impossible. *She needed to work.* Needed to dive into a bigger screen than her laptop. Computers had been her salvation; submerging in the 'wired world' was where she could disappear, her rioting emotions calmed by the occupation of her mind. *Her computer friends would never let her down or betray her.*

Sophie grabbed a light parka against the cool night air, her back-pack, and her weapon. The dogs she resettled on her bed with a treat.

She'd get caught up at the office. Then, by the time Jake and Felicia rolled in to work, she'd be prepared. All business. Able to act like she didn't care that Felicia was sleeping over, whether it was platonic or a sex marathon.

Sophie got into her Security Solutions SUV and headed for the office. The dark was her friend, as it had always been.

CHAPTER THIRTY-FOUR

THE BITCH IS BACK.

Akane set aside the phone that had pinged him awake with a text from his spy. He reached down for his pants. He had to move fast, before extra security or one of her boyfriends showed up.

"Where ya going, baby?" Sleepy voice from the other side of the bed. "Stay with me. We can have some more fun."

Akane glanced over at the naked woman beside him. Makeup had run, circling her eyes, along with a purple mark from his hand. The whore had bruises around her throat, too, and she was still looking for more? *He was definitely going to see her again.* His groin stirred, but he shook his head. He peeled a couple of C-notes off his bankroll and dropped them on the nightstand. "Be gone before I get back. I'll call you."

Akane dressed rapidly, picked up his weapons, and left.

He had spies keeping an eye on all the comings and goings of his targets, and he mulled over Terence's visit to Security Solutions the day before. *What could Terence be playing at?* He was probably trying to get their team to help him while setting them up at the same time.

Terence thought he was so smart—and Akane would let him think so, all the way until the end.

He'd gloated over a secret button camera he'd installed to watch Terence discover his uncle's body. Chopping Terence's surrogate father up like that had been disgusting and a lot of work, but Terence's horror, the way he'd puked and cried…worth every messy minute.

"You killed my family, Terence," Akane muttered. "You're never going to be done suffering until I finally end your miserable life."

Akane arrived at the office building and made a pass, driving by at the speed limit, checking out the situation. The bitch had parked her car around the corner, but a light was on in the third-floor office. He smiled. She'd never see him coming.

This was going to be fun.

CHAPTER THIRTY-FIVE

Sophie cracked her knuckles as Amara, Jinjai, and Ying, her faithful computer friends, replicated through several incarnations now, whirred into life in the little computer lab Connor had set up. The streets of Hilo had been quiet and deserted on the way into the office; she hadn't seen a soul. She'd already verified that the Security Solutions outer office door was locked and alarmed, but she could still hear Marcella's voice in her head, scolding her for coming in alone, at night, with Akane still on the loose.

Still, she felt safe in the locked, armed, quiet office—and a loaded Glock rested on the desk beside her in case of surprises.

Sophie needed her wired world. *Craved it.*

A lumpy white envelope marked *SOPHIE* in Jake's bold handwriting was set beside her inbox tray. Sophie ripped it open and took out a stick drive.

Must be some data she needed to analyze for one of their cases.

Shaking off the angst about Jake, she plugged in the drive and loaded her programs. She put on her headphones, piping in a Mozart concerto to get herself in the right mental space. When the computers were done activating, the first order of business was checking

DAVID, her rogue data analysis program, for any evidence collected on Akane's whereabouts.

DAVID came online. The rogue data mining software had been set to monitor keywords related to Akane Chang. She was disappointed to see that the collection cache was empty. That psychopath knew about Security Solutions' strength with online and computer monitoring. He had been staying off the grid and out of public view, likely hidden by his allies. He must be using only cash and seldom going anywhere.

Sophie opened the contents of the stick drive and discovered a spreadsheet of names and addresses. The whole document revolved around a family tree focusing on Terry and Healani Chang and their siblings and descendants. The spreadsheet included not only the Chang family clan, complete with full names, addresses and contact information, but allies and associates. Colors and symbols in a key on the side, designated affiliations and functions within the family business.

Sophie grinned—this information was going to be invaluable in tracking Akane's whereabouts and the Chang operation in general.

Sophie dug in, dragging and dropping names into DAVID for more data mining. By the time she was done sorting the contents of this stick drive, she'd know more about the Chang operation on the Big Island than anyone ever had.

A terrible shattering of glass as the window near her broke was Sophie's first inkling that something was amiss. The air filled with the sharp smell of a canister of tear gas. Yellowish smoke belched from the canister as it rolled across the floor to bump into the wheels of her office chair.

Sophie tore off her headphones, grabbed the Glock, and rolled out of her chair to take cover beside her desk. Vapor belched out into the small space of the room, stinging her eyes and filling the air in billowing clouds. Sophie held her breath, shutting her eyes, trying to remember the distance to the door. *She had to get it open and get out!*

Sophie ripped off her shirt and covered her nose and mouth, blinking burning eyes as she crawled toward the door, the Glock in one hand and the shirt held over her face with the other.

The louvered covering over the window flew inward. Glass sprayed Sophie as the rest of the window was bashed in. Sophie shut her eyes, held her breath, and got her cloth-covered hand on the lever-style door handle. She heaved downward desperately, hearing the thud of boots landing on the floor behind her.

"Where do you think you're going, bitch?" *Akane.* She'd recognize that voice anywhere, even when muffled by a gas mask.

A hand in Sophie's hair yanked her back from the door and another yank landed her on her ass.

Sophie brought the Glock up and fired, aiming backward, shooting blind.

The report in the enclosed space deafened her, and the grip on her hair, straining her neck as her head was pulled back, didn't loosen. *She'd missed!*

Sophie inadvertently inhaled. Instantly coughing, her lungs felt on fire. Her eyes stung in spite of being closed, and a blow to her head stunned her. The weapon was wrenched out of her hand.

"I should just shoot you right now, but that would be too easy. I want to finish what we started in the jungle," Akane said. "You've caused me a lot of hassles, and it's payback time."

She could breathe later.

Now was time for an all-out effort to escape, or die trying.

Sophie drew her feet underneath her buttocks and threw herself forward to stand, ripping her hair out of Akane's hand. She was scarcely aware of her stinging scalp as she pitched forward, crashing against the door, her hands scrabbling for the handle. This time it opened. Sophie fell through the doorway, landing to roll to her feet. Her diaphragm spasmed, demanding a breath, and she cracked her eyes open enough to aim herself in a dive, landing behind Felicia's desk in the main reception area.

Foul vapor billowed out of the computer lab in pursuit, but

Sophie pulled Felicia's sweater down off of her chair and grabbed a couple of gasping breaths. Holding the fabric over her face, she groped for the alarm button they'd had installed on the bottom of the receptionist's desk. She pressed it repeatedly.

Akane cursed and his boots thundered as he followed her out of the computer lab. She shut her eyes against the tear gas and wedged herself in under the desk, preparing to make him work to get her out.

"You must be Akane Chang." Pim Wat's cool, composed voice came from the main office doorway. "I've been looking for you."

Pim Wat? Here? Now? Sophie couldn't believe what she was hearing.

Sophie pulled the sweater away from her face enough to squint through streaming eyes at a small, dark figure standing silhouetted in the doorway.

"Who the hell are you?" Akane sounded outraged.

"Sophie's mother. You've been a problem for her long enough." A unique sound: *bap! bap! bap!*

Shots from a silenced weapon.

Even with her eyes shut, Sophie could picture where Pim Wat had shot Akane: two to the chest, one to the head. *Her mother was a pro.*

"He's probably wearing a vest, Mother," Sophie rasped between coughs. "Make sure you get him."

"Oh, I got him. And now, let's clear the air in this place." Pim Wat ran forward and shut the computer lab door, trapping most of the gas inside the small room, turned on an overhead fan, and opened the windows of the other offices as Sophie kept her eyes shut and focused on breathing through the sweater.

Sophie waited until she felt her mother's cool hand on her shoulder. "Sophie Malee. Are you injured?"

"Just some gas inhalation." Now that the crisis was passing, Sophie could also feel her scalp burning—she'd definitely lost a patch of hair to Akane's grip. "I pressed an alarm. The police are on their way." She could already hear the wail of sirens in the distance.

"We'll catch up later, then." Pim Wat dropped the weapon, a silenced SIG, into Sophie's lap. "You can thank me and return my weapon when the police are done with it. I was never here."

Sophie blinked stinging eyes until she could make out Akane, flat on his back, his arms sprawled. Red pulp filled the gas mask where his face had been. Yes, Pim Wat had got him.

When she looked up, Pim Wat had vanished, shutting the office door behind her.

CHAPTER THIRTY-SIX

Day Eighteen

JAKE WOKE at the blaring ringtone he used for the Security Solutions big boss, Sheldon Hamilton. Outside the sliding glass windows of his apartment's deck, the barest hint of dawn pinkened the sky as his boss yelled that Sophie had been attacked by Akane Chang in their office downtown. "Where the hell were you, Jake? Where was your security detail?" Hamilton ranted. "And what the hell are you doing in your bed while your pregnant girlfriend is at work downtown, dealing with a serial killer?"

Jake's heart jackhammered. He rolled over and reached for his pants, catching Felicia's sleepy, alarmed gaze as she blinked at him. Jake had never heard Hamilton raise his voice before, let alone yell. "Slow down, Hamilton. I'm getting dressed and I'll be there in five minutes."

"Thank God she was able to deal with Chang herself, no thanks to you. That bastard threw a tear gas grenade through the window and came in from the outside." Hamilton was breathing heavily. "The police are crawling all over the office. They've taken Sophie in for questioning, since she shot him execution style—two to the chest, one in the head. Get your ass down to the South Hilo PD station. I've already called Security Solutions' lawyer. I'm almost there myself." Hamilton hung up abruptly.

Jake struggled to get his pants up over his booted foot. He stood, tripping as he tried to get his shirt on. "Shit!"

"I'm sorry," Felicia said. "I should have woken you up when Sophie came by."

Jake got his head through the neck of the shirt at last. "Sophie came by?"

"Yeah. Around two a.m. She was looking for you." Felicia flushed. "I told her you were sleeping and she said she'd see you later. I should've just woken you up, but you were finally asleep, and she said it was okay."

"She must have thought... Oh my God, no wonder she went down to the office in the middle of the night." Fury darkened Jake's vision. "Get out, Felicia. Damn it to hell!"

"Hey! No call to take that tone, old man," Felicia said, but hurried to grab her purse and exit.

Jake raked a hand through his hair and cursed. He grabbed his crutch, weapon, wallet, and keys, and headed for the Security Solutions SUV.

Guilt gnawed at Jake's gut as he navigated the early morning streets of Hilo.

If only he'd just gone in and woken Sophie up... If only he hadn't dismissed the security team! He'd sent them home after work, planning to spend the night with Sophie and not wanting an audience for their reunion. But when he'd unlocked Sophie's door after work and seen her sleeping, the dogs curled up on the bed with her, he'd changed his mind.

He'd wanted to join her. Had curled his hands into fists to keep from touching her.

But she was pregnant, and she needed her rest.

And he needed a little more time to figure out where to go from the stalemate they were stuck in, waiting on news about the baby's parentage.

Jake had taken the coward's way out, and left.

He'd gone back to his apartment, figuring he'd see her in the morning. He'd eaten pizza with Felicia when she showed up with a big meat lover's special. He'd taken his pain meds and fallen asleep while Felicia was still watching TV.

All of that was true, and innocent, but damning nonetheless, because it added up to not being there for Sophie. If they'd been together, if she hadn't been upset, she'd never have gone to the office alone. There was no denying, even to himself, that he'd made choices—and they'd almost cost her life.

But she'd made choices too!

"Damn fool thing to do, going in there alone," he muttered, pulling up and parking at the South Hilo police station's strip mall parking lot. "Damn it, Sophie, you have another life to watch out for, now!"

The baby had begun to feel real to him, someone to be protected and cared for. He worried about the baby—because even if it wasn't his...*it was hers.*

Jake waited in his car outside the police station, knowing there was nowhere but the tiny doorway reception area to sit inside. He went through his isometric seat workout, discharging tension through exercise as he always had. Then he paced back and forth in the deserted parking lot on his crutch, watching dawn bleed up and listening to the waking mynahs and doves, and the last of the coqui frog chorus.

He whirled around as the door of the police station opened.

Hamilton had his arm around Sophie as the pair exited. Sophie looked gray with exhaustion, and Hamilton's sharp dark eyes, behind those hipster glasses, flicked over Jake with contempt.

"Sophie." Jake ignored Hamilton and hobbled forward, tossing his crutch aside, pulling her into a hug. "I'm so glad you're okay."

She stood stiffly in his arms, her hands at her sides. She smelled of the tear gas bomb, and the sweat of fear and exertion. With his cheek close to her hair, he spotted an oozing patch of bare scalp that had to hurt. Little bits of glass were still caught in her hair, sparkling like snowflakes. "It's over now. He's dead," she whispered.

"You have to tell me what happened." Jake moved back, holding Sophie's arms, trying to get eye contact. She stared down at the boot on his leg.

"I'm really tired. I just want to get a shower and go to bed."

"I need to know…" He couldn't seem to let go of her.

"What you need doesn't matter, Dunn. We'll have a meeting tomorrow to go over everything. Chang's killing looks enough like self-defense for the cops to let her go for now. I'm having a medical team meet us at the jet to check Sophie out and make sure she's okay. Bix will contact you with the time and location for our meeting, since the office is a crime scene." Hamilton rewrapped his arm around Sophie's shoulder and tugged her against his side posses-sively. *Was Hamilton making a move on Sophie?* Had something developed between them while they spent all that time together on Kaua`i?

Jake's brows drew together as Sophie went unresisting with their boss toward a Security Solutions SUV driven by Thom Tang. Sophie looked back over her shoulder. "Please don't forget to take care of the dogs," she said.

Jake's fists clenched but he made himself smile reassuringly. "Don't worry about a thing. They'll be waiting for you. And so will I."

Jake had to watch as their boss helped her tenderly into the back of the SUV and got in beside her, and Thom drove them away.

CHAPTER THIRTY-SEVEN

Day Nineteen

Sophie rubbed the scar on her cheek. The ridged line of the skin graft that ran up over her artificial cheekbone felt numb, yet tingly under her fingers, as it always did. She looked around Dr. Wilson's office, her gaze tracking over the familiar surroundings. The leather couch she sat on. The psychologist in her comfortable-looking lounger. The plain wood coffee table with its round ceramic sand tray, little rake, and bowl of clay figures. Amateurish paintings on the walls, seascapes mostly. *Probably done by a client.*

"My son did those paintings." Dr. Wilson must have been tracking Sophie's gaze—and reading her mind, too, as she often seemed able to.

Dr. Wilson wore a turquoise-colored wrap dress and a small, sparkly gem on a chain at her throat. Her blonde hair was tousled perfection brushing her shoulders, and her blue eyes were filled with worried compassion. "It's been too long, Sophie. I understand from Connor, who called to get this emergency appointment, that you shot Akane Chang yesterday."

"Pim Wat shot him." Sophie hadn't meant to say it so immediately and baldly, but relief followed the confession. *Dr. Wilson knew everything already; Dr. Wilson and Connor were the only people she had no secrets from.* "Mother broke into the office during the attack and shot him. I'm not sure what would have happened if she hadn't."

Dr. Wilson blinked. "Why did you lie and say that you did it? To the cops, to Hamilton?"

"Pim Wat dropped the gun into my lap. Said she'd see me later, and that she had never been there." Sophie blew out a breath. "It never occurred to me to tell them she'd done it."

"We need to talk about why you automatically covered for Pim Wat, and if that's the best thing for *you*," Dr. Wilson said. "But first, let's go back in time a bit. I'm glad we were able to have a phone session while you were on Kaua'i, but I feel way behind the eight ball, as usual. Catch me up to what prompted you to go into the office late at night, alone." The psychologist's brows drew together in a frown. "That doesn't seem to have been the best idea."

"I know. But I was upset. Jake was with Felicia instead of with me." Sophie described the series of events. "I believe her, that they didn't…do anything. But clearly, while I was gone on Kaua'i and Jake was injured, they developed some kind of relationship. She is infatuated with him."

"Oh dear. And he chose to let you sleep instead of joining you, and then hung out with his gal pal or whatever she's become." Dr. Wilson pointed her pen at Sophie. "Kind of like what Connor is to you."

"Connor is no gal pal with movies and pizza. He is…" Sophie twisted her fingers together, unable to come up with words to describe Connor's unwavering commitment. "Connor is the only one who is unequivocally supporting me. He's been there for me, no matter who I've slept with. Last night—or I should say, yesterday morning—when the police let me out of the station, I was totally dead on my feet. Jake tried to talk to me after the attack, but I just didn't have the strength to get through the discussions I know we need to have. Connor knew that, too. He fended Jake off and took me

202

to the jet. Had a doctor come and assess me there." Sophie smiled. "The doctor even brought a portable sonogram machine. I saw my baby for the first time."

"Oh, my dear. How was that?"

"Just…magic." Sophie shut her eyes a moment, remembering her first sight of the tiny, curled, shrimplike shape of the child in her womb as the cool, gel-covered sonogram wand slid over her abdomen. She'd been gripping Connor's hand, and he'd squeezed hers back, so hard it hurt. "The baby is healthy. The heartbeat was normal. We even saw it move."

"Could you tell what sex it was?"

"Perhaps the doctor could, but I told him I didn't want to know." Sophie sighed. "Connor kissed me as we were watching the baby on the monitor. I let him; it felt right. We were sharing such an important moment."

"Connor's participating with you when neither of the possible fathers have stepped up to get involved," Dr. Wilson said. "He seems to genuinely care about the baby, from what you've described, both on Kaua`i and in this situation. Be careful, though, that you don't mistake his motivations. He's in love with you and is using this vulnerable time in your life to get closer to you. Become indispensable."

"I know." Sophie looked down at her hands. "And I'm not going to lie and say it hasn't been working." She shook her head. "I mean, I still don't have any sexual feelings for him. But I trust him again, after all he's done to make up for that other thing."

"Can you forgive and forget what he did in faking his death?" Dr. Wilson's brows shot up. "Don't you think he showed his priorities through that situation?"

"I think priorities can change. Perhaps the Ghost isn't as important to him as it once was." Sophie sighed again. "I don't know. But I do know Alika was definitely different toward me on Kaua`i, and I can't blame him. The adjustments he's going through with the loss of his arm are huge. Whatever we had before seems gone. On both sides. I only feel a kind of…brotherly friendship for him. The possibility of the baby being his just seemed like a complication to him, I could tell. He had me over for a family dinner, but showed no interest in spending time with me otherwise while I was on Kaua`i. I loved meeting all of his Hawaiian relatives, though."

"And Jake? Jake is the most likely candidate as the baby's father, condoms or no condoms." Dr. Wilson smiled. "Just in terms of sheer frequency of opportunity, as it were."

A blush heated Sophie's neck. "That much is true. I missed Jake terribly. I wanted to see him the minute I got back. Experiencing what I did with Felicia's involvement with Jake, whatever is going on with them, has made me understand jealousy so much more. I wanted to rip her hair out by the roots when she answered his door." Sophie shook her head. "Jake is obviously conflicted. He has always been jealous. Being a father to Alika's child, if it goes that way, might well be too much for him." She described the issues Jake had told her about with his own father's lying, cheating, and ultimate abandonment. "He has a sensitivity beyond the norm about secrets. Betrayal. It's always been an issue for us, because there's so much I can't tell him."

"And there always will be."

"And there always will be," Sophie agreed.

"What an interesting conundrum. I wonder how all of this will resolve." Dr. Wilson's gaze was calm and compassionate.

"Interesting? Ha. Easy for you to describe it that way." Sophie smiled. "But I know this: my baby and I will be okay no matter what happens. I'm going to be a mother. And I'm very happy about that."

"Good." Dr. Wilson smiled back. "Let's circle back around to Pim Wat. Why did you lie about who shot Akane? Why didn't you tell the police that a woman broke into the office and killed him?"

"How could I possibly explain that? Pim Wat had used lock picks or her own key on the door; there were no signs of forced entry. Why would some unknown woman show up just in time and kill my attacker? It would just seem like I was lying, because of course, she was also wearing gloves." Sophie rubbed her cheek again, closing her eyes. "Believe me. I considered my options as I was sitting there, looking at Akane's body, with that hot pistol in my lap. I came up with an explanation for her weapon: it was a backup I'd hidden, taped under Felicia's desk after he disarmed me in the computer lab."

Dr. Wilson digested this. "I worry that, now that you've lied for Pim Wat, she has leverage on you." Dr. Wilson's blue eyes were intent. "How did Pim Wat know Akane was going to attack you? Why did she do what she did? There are so many unanswered questions about your mother's role."

"She has killed to protect me before. She shot the assassin who was hired to kill me by the Changs." Sophie reiterated Pim Wat's story about shooting the assassin she called the Lizard. "She is a strange sort of guardian angel, watching over me."

"Perhaps her way of showing love is eliminating those who threaten you."

"She does not love me in any normal sense," Sophie stated definitely. "She is territorial. I belong to her, and no one gets to mess with what belongs to her. She complained of the challenge of the Lizard, of taking a bullet in the vest for me when he tried to kill her —so I know what she does is not always easy. Perhaps that's why I covered for her. To honor that."

Dr. Wilson snorted. "She may not love you in any normal sense, but you are her daughter. You do love her, and a part of you was both loyal and grateful for what she'd done in saving your life and shooting Akane."

Sophie said nothing.

"Well, let's hope your story of having a backup gun stashed under Felicia's desk holds up, and covering for her doesn't bite you on the butt."

"That's not the only worry I have about my mother." Sophie told Dr. Wilson about the strange and wonderful visit from her childhood nanny. "Armita was just the same—and seeing her, I felt just the same about her. She *was* my mother for the first seven years of my life, in everything but name. I asked her to join me, to help me care for my baby—but even though she seemed thrilled with the idea, she also seemed afraid of my mother. Too afraid to try to leave, or even for me to let Pim Wat know that I'd seen her."

"Armita obviously came to you at great personal risk, if Pim Wat has prevented her from seeing you all of these years." Dr. Wilson shook her head. "And she took that risk solely to warn you."

"Yes. I hope I did the right thing, telling her I was pregnant. I hope she won't tell Pim Wat. I do not trust my mother." Sophie wrapped her arms over her abdomen. "She has plans for me. And a child may not be part of them."

"Unfortunately, I don't think you've seen the last of your mother, nor do we know what her real agenda is." Dr. Wilson made a note on her tablet. "Now, what are you going to do about Jake?"

Sophie shook her head. "I don't know. I just don't know."

CHAPTER THIRTY-EIGHT

AUNTY GRACE POURED Terence a cup of fragrant green tea with only a little tremor in her hands. "Mahalo, Aunty." Once his great-aunt's tea was poured and she'd sipped, Terence lifted the simple clay cup to his lips as well. "Appreciate you meeting with me."

Grace Kapuniokalani Chang Manuka Rivera was the oldest surviving Chang, and Terence's deceased namesake grandfather's aunt. Aunty Grace had outlived two husbands and a couple of wars, and she was still a power player, owning a majority of shares in Chang Enterprises, Inc., the family's umbrella company. Grace had just successfully blocked his renaming of that company with her share vote.

"What a surprise you turned out to be, Terence Chang." Morning sunlight came through the window of her living room to light Grace's white hair like a halo. "What am I to do about you?"

Terence hadn't visited Grace until after Akane's death because he wasn't sure whose side she was on. Though he'd heard through the "coconut wireless" that Grace was in favor of the kind of progressive change toward legitimate business that Terence wanted to foster, Akane was one of her grandsons, and Terence had just eliminated an entire branch of her family tree.

Terence set his cup down on the table. "I hope you will support me in taking the company in a different direction. There's a board meeting in an hour."

"And how glad I am that I wasn't at that last meeting," Grace said.

Terence closed his mouth on the impulse to apologize.

He'd killed one of her sons, his wife, one of her grandsons and a niece—and this morning they'd had the news of Akane's death, too. She had no more living family from that son. How could he ever apologize?

"It didn't have to go down that way," Terence said instead.

"I agree with you about that." Grace set down her cup, but her age-spotted hands still held it tightly as if seeking warmth. "You surprised all of us that day, Terence, by showing that you have what it takes to lead. However, I want you to know…you won't be leading this family alone." She reached in the capacious pocket of her hibiscus-patterned muumuu and withdrew a cell phone. She tapped the screen and held the phone up for Terence to see.

An oddly angled video began to play, and Terence jerked in shock as he recognized himself, seated at the head of the plastic-covered conference table. *Someone had videoed the whole massacre!* Emma was supposed to have collected all the cell phones, but clearly one had been missed.

Aunty Grace turned the video off when it reached the point where Terence drew his pistol. "You'll forgive me if I don't play the section where you murder my family. I've already seen it too many times."

Terence blew out a shaky breath. "I'm truly sorry, Aunty Grace." If it made him weak to apologize, if it made her angrier to hear his feeble words—there was nothing more to lose, at this point. *She had a video of him committing murder!*

"I've had long enough to think about this situation from all angles. To consider your track record, and to think about how you set up that meeting and what you did there. I concluded that you did what you did because you could not see Akane take the lead in the family. Sad as it is for me to admit, you are not the only one who knew that Akane's leadership would ultimately be the end of us, and my son would always have backed him. If you hadn't taken steps, I would have." Grace set the phone down. "I accept that you didn't want to kill my son and his family. That you took no pleasure in it. That you may not want to lead Chang Enterprises, even now—but that you are the best person to do so. I accept all of that." She raised her eyes to meet his, and they were so dark he couldn't see a pupil in their obsidian depths. "But hear this, nephew. I accept, but I will never forget. This video is stored in the Cloud and will be sent to the police if you ever cross me. I will be your silent partner in every major Chang Enterprises decision going forward." She took a sip of tea, and her hands were perfectly steady. "Do we understand each other?"

"We do." Terence picked up his teacup and lifted it in toast, hoping that his hand didn't shake either. "I will benefit greatly from your wisdom, Aunty."

TERENCE LOOKED around the long koa table in the conference room at the downtown warehouse of Chang Enterprises, Inc. All of the remaining family members had gathered for the first board meeting since his hostile takeover.

"I don't see any plastic on the floor," his cousin Leo Chang said. "That's the only reason I came all the way into the room." A nervous titter from the rest of the group met this sally.

"Those ugly days are behind us," Terence said. "I hope everyone is with me, going forward, now that we've cleared out the negative elements."

"And you're not the negative element?" Penny Chang, his PR manager cousin, was a known Akane sympathizer. "You seem like one to me, what with the mass murder of family members and all."

Another edgy titter. Emma, stationed by the exit, picked up a shotgun leaning against the wall and racked it with a harsh sound. She'd been elected peacekeeper for the day and was dressed like a dominatrix in black leather and high-heeled boots.

"I never wanted things to go down the way they did," Terence said. "But you all know what Akane was. The transition after Byron has been rough, but believe me when I tell you, I am the lesser of two evils."

"And if that was all you were, Terence…" Aunty Grace spoke up. "But I think you are much more than the lesser of evils."

There were several ways that statement could be interpreted.

Terence held his breath. His hand slid down and his fingers curled around the grip of a pistol taped to the table's underside. He'd walked in with the rest of the family and ostentatiously surrendered his phone and weapons, but that didn't mean he hadn't taken out some insurance beforehand.

"You are much more than a lesser choice of any kind. You are smart, college-educated, and a successful businessman in your own right. You are what we need to take this company and this family out of the shadows, the back alleys, the corner drug deals—and bring us into the light." Grace looked around the table, her dark eyes boring into each person. "I look forward to a day when the Changs not only own the Big Island, we run it—from legitimate positions of power as elected county officials, on advisory boards, and as majority share-holders in growing businesses. I look forward to a day when we can stop hiding, ashamed that we run gambling and whores and make meth. We're better than that! And with Terence leading us, we can do more and be more." She took a sip of water. "No one lost more than I did at that last board meeting. And if I can get past the death of my son and his family to see the bigger picture, you can too. Besides, I'll be right beside Terence, making sure he does this right." Aunty Grace smacked a hand down on the table emphatically, and everyone jumped.

A loud murmur that definitely had a positive tone filled the room as the family processed this.

Terence inclined his head to Grace. "I will do all that I can to earn your confidence. Now, if each of you will direct your attention to the agenda? It's been updated since our last meeting, and we have a number of items to go over."

Aunty Grace's clout had steamrolled the last of the resistance. Terence and the family got down to new business.

CHAPTER THIRTY-NINE

Sᴏᴘʜɪᴇ ᴡᴏᴋᴇ to the hairy warmth and rumbling snores of Ginger and Tank, taking up half of the bed. She rolled over to look out through the sliding glass doors at dawn coming up across the smooth glass of early morning Hilo Bay. Birds were waking in the banyan tree outside, and the last of the coqui frog chorus was dying down as morning lit the sky. She pillowed her cheek on her hands, gratitude and well-being filling her.

She was sleeping without blackout drapes. The depression was better, at least temporarily. And she was going to have a baby, a child of her own to love.

She'd returned late in the evening yesterday from her appointment with Dr. Wilson to find the dogs in her apartment, and a note from Jake: *"Took them out for a walk and they've been fed. Please call me as soon as you're ready to talk."*

Sophie had already decided that she wasn't going to be ready to talk until she knew the baby's paternity; whatever conclusion they might come to before that might be changed by that news.

Maybe it was time to call the clinic instead of just waiting for an email.

She'd gone to bed early after a simple meal of canned soup, and this morning her tummy was growling with hunger, not morning sickness. "Let's go for a run, dogs, and I'll take you out to breakfast."

It wasn't long before Sophie, Ginger, and Tank were jogging through the park. Sophie felt good today: energetic, strong. The faint sting of the bald patch on her scalp rubbing against the inside of her ball cap was the only reminder of recent ugly events.

And today, she wasn't going to focus on ugly events. She was going to enjoy running with her dogs in the park and feeling good for once.

Sophie remembered that first glimpse of the tiny shape on the sonogram and felt that excitement and anticipation all over again. *She was going to be a mother!* She was still glad about this unexpected miracle, even with all its challenges.

What names would be good? Dad would have ideas. Perhaps something that harked back to her grandparents, gone too soon in a flu epidemic when her father was young.

What would it be like to hold her baby? To feed it?

Some things seemed impossible to imagine, even as worries crowded in—how could she work, and provide care for an infant?

Too many questions. Not enough answers. Worrying wouldn't solve anything; it just stole any happiness she could have now.

"A useless emotion. Like guilt," Sophie murmured aloud, remembering Connor telling her not to bother with useless emotions.

Sophie tied the dogs to a post outside the same modest restaurant where she and Alika had eaten breakfast not long ago; she still remembered telling him about her relationship with Jake, and later finding him doing a martial arts routine alone in the alley.

So many things had happened since then.

Sophie got a table right next to the window and fetched water in a bowl for the dogs, before settling in to eat a hearty breakfast, thankful that her digestive system was cooperating.

On the way back to her apartment, walking through the park, she called the clinic on Oahu that was performing the paternity test. The clerk on call established her identity, and then passed her on to one of the technicians.

"Hello, Ms. Ang. Yes, I'm glad to hear from you. I was just putting together your report and getting ready to contact you."

Sophie's heart pounded and she put her hand on her chest, drawing a deep breath. "Please do get that report into the mail for me. But, since I have you on the phone, do you mind giving me the information now?"

"Certainly." Keys clicked as the woman worked her computer. "The results came in with a 98% probability that Alika Wolcott is the father of your child."

"Thank you," Sophie said faintly, and ended the call.

CHAPTER FORTY

ALIKA WAS WORKING with his physical therapist, learning to tie a shoelace one-handed.

"Be patient. Make a loop. Pin the lace to your shoe with your thumb. Use your fingers to circle the lace around and through the loop."

"I can just get Velcro shoes," Alika grumbled.

Sandy Pitman, his physical therapist, quirked a brow. "You never know when you'll have to tie something."

Alika kept swinging his stump arm forward. He could still feel the arm as if it were there, could not stop the impulse of his ghost hand from trying to assist. The fingers of his right hand fumbled and felt too large for the task, but he'd just seen the PT perform it one-handed, so it could be done.

Alika persisted, but finally, when he tugged on the tail of the lace, the whole thing melted into a tangle. He swore. "This shouldn't be so freakin' hard. A kid can do this. I want to punch something."

"We'll get to the punching bag later. Your reward for getting this figured out." The attractive female PT had been in Iraq, and she was missing both legs from the knees down. Alika couldn't even grumble that the woman didn't understand his struggle, his anger, the way even the simplest things that a child could perform had become difficult challenges—when watching Sandy arrange herself to stand gave him a zing of compassion.

Alika's phone, stashed in the loose pocket of his workout shorts, vibrated. He didn't usually answer it during therapy, but he needed a break. "Excuse me."

He straightened up and walked away, feeling a flicker of gratitude that he could still do that, that at least his legs were strong and whole. "Alika here."

"Alika, it's Sophie. I have news about the paternity test." Sophie's voice was flat, uninflected.

Alika froze. *Trust Sophie to cut to the chase without even a greeting!*

Sophie's pregnancy news had been too difficult to assimilate in the midst of his personal turmoil; he'd managed to compartmentalize it and put it out of his mind. The only thing he'd been really clear on when Sophie visited was that, while he'd always care for her as a friend, he wasn't "in love" with her since the bomb had blown them apart.

He felt bad he'd almost forgotten about the situation. "Are you all right? Feeling okay?"

"I am fine." She paused. "And you're the father."

"What?" Alika put his ghost arm out to grab the wall and ended up crashing into it. "You're kidding, right?"

"I'm afraid not. The clinic says it's a 98% probability that we're having a child together." Sophie sounded stiff, wooden, how she got when she was struggling or uncomfortable. "But like I told you. You aren't obligated. This is my baby and I'll raise it and care for it myself."

A powerful wave of emotion blasted through Alika at those words. "No way are you shutting me out."

Not like his dad had done to his mom, refusing even to acknowledge that Alika was his son. *This was a chance to do things the way he wished they'd been done for him.* The irony that Alika had accidentally fathered a child, when he'd so hated being a bastard himself, made him rub his eyes, overwhelmed.

Sophie drew a shuddering breath. "Are you telling me you want to be involved?"

"Hell yes. What do you need? Say the word. Want to stay here, at my house? My family and I would love to have you. I showed you the room you and the baby can have." Alika straightened up from the wall. "We're doing this together. I might only have one arm, but that arm can still hold a baby."

Sophie sniffed audibly. "I appreciate that. I don't need anything, but I do need someone to talk over all the decisions I have to make. Like what kind of doctor to get, and what kind of delivery to have." Her voice trailed off. "There's a lot to learn."

"I admit I'm no expert on pregnancy and parenting. I'll have to get some books and read up on it. But I'll do whatever I can to help and support you. "

"Thanks, Alika. It's been hard dealing with this alone."

"Jake? He's not...there for you?" It felt awkward to ask Sophie about her relationship with the man she'd chosen over him—but it didn't even sting this time. Hopefully, Jake would step up. Sophie needed someone to love on her through this, and it wasn't going to be him.

"Jake's had a hard time with the idea that he might not be the baby's father. I don't know if we'll be able to get past this. You being the father, I mean." Sophie's voice wobbled.

"Ah, shit." Alika waved Sandy away as the PT approached, mouthing "emergency" as he strode to the back door of his home gym. Once outside, he took a restorative look at the beautiful backdrop of Namolokama, Mamaloa, and Hihimanu, the three stunning green mountains that cupped Hanalei Bay in their arms. "I'm sorry, Sophie. I hope you guys can work it out. We never talked about it, but my feelings changed after the bomb."

"I knew things were different between us when I saw you on Kaua`i. Not that the arm thing mattered to me. It wasn't that."

"I know it wasn't. It was the whole situation." Alika rubbed his eyes again. "Did you know I had a ring in my pocket when I met you in your dad's lobby? I was going to ask you to marry me. I thought I'd wait until we were on the elevator and then I'd pop the question when we were alone." He hadn't meant to tell her that. *Ever.* Strangely, it didn't hurt to do so now.

"Oh, Alika." Sophie's voice had gone thick and husky.

"What would you have answered?"

"No. No, I can't marry you. That's what I would have said." Sophie was definitely crying. "I think I'm in love with Jake."

"And yet here we are. Having a child together." He sighed. "I'll still marry you—for the child's sake. If you want to."

"No, Alika. But thanks. This is so sad." The phone line crackled as Sophie sniffled. "I'm in the park with the dogs, sitting on a bench. People are looking at me, and I just want to blow my nose on my shirt."

"If you were here, I'd give you my best one-armed hug."

"And I'm sure it's better than most men's two-armed hugs." She sighed. "I'll call you, because I'm going to have to pick a delivery team, and I need help with that."

"You know my number. Tattoo it on your forehead."

"I don't think so. Phone numbers change too often."

Alika laughed. "You crack me up. Always so literal. I'm going to be a dad, Sophie." Joy bloomed somewhere deep inside him. "I'm going to be a dad!"

"And I'm going to be a mother. It's still hard to believe, even though I've seen the baby on a sonogram. I'll send you the photo."

Alika's heart speeded up at the thought of actually seeing his child. "Is it a girl or a boy?"

"I asked not to know. I want to be surprised. I hope that's okay."

"I'd like that, too. And I can't wait to see the photo."

A comfortable silence stretched between them. Alika shut his eyes, feeling the warm breeze, listening to the rattle of the coconut palm fronds, the shush of the wind in the bamboo landscaping around the pool. His mom and grandma were going to go apeshit with excitement. They wouldn't care that he and Sophie weren't together as long as everyone was getting along and the baby was healthy. "I want you and Jake to work things out. Tell Jake that from me, will you?"

"I wish I didn't have to tell him this news," Sophie whispered. "I don't know how he's going to take it."

"I want you to be happy, but if Jake can't see how lucky he is, then we're better off without him."

"I'm happy about the baby, regardless," Sophie said.

"Me too. Let's do this. Let's figure out how to be parents."

CHAPTER FORTY-ONE

AFTER THE PHONE call to Alika, Sophie sent Jake a brief text message. *"We need to talk. Call me ASAP."*

She had to deliver the news about the baby's parentage in person —and she had to tell Jake what she should have told him a while ago: somewhere along the way, she'd fallen in love with him.

She missed him. Wanted to be with him.

And she hoped like hell he hadn't already moved on with the pretty, smart, unencumbered Felicia.

Sophie looked around the park as she slid her phone into her pocket. Old men and young children were fishing off the jetty. Mynah birds hopped on the smooth grass, and palm trees swished overhead. The dogs had curled up, snuggled against each other, tired of waiting for her to get off the phone. She stood up and tweaked their leashes. "Let's go."

Sophie walked along the curving concrete pathway this time, too full from the large breakfast for running. She tipped her face back, enjoying the sunshine.

Relief that she and Alika were in accord filled her with well-being. It was so sweet that he'd proposed for the baby's sake; he was that kind of man, and his excitement about the baby was a huge load off her shoulders. Whatever happened with Jake, between Connor and Alika, she'd have all the support she'd need in the coming months.

What was Connor going to think of this latest development?

Sophie paused, leaning against a palm tree, and texted him. *"Got the results back from the clinic. Alika is the baby's father. I talked with him via phone and he is happy about it and plans to be involved."* She paused, nibbling on her lip. *"We both agree we are not getting together romantically. But I am going to try to reconcile with Jake."* Again, she paused, imagining Connor's face as he read the messages, the blow to hopes he'd never verbalized. *"I appreciate all you've done, and I hope our friendship will continue, unchanged."*

That certainly put it out there, and it was a measure of how much things had improved between them that she hated to hurt Connor like this—but it was better just to tell him. The pregnancy already took most of her internal and external energy.

She slid her phone back into her pocket and this time moved into a gentle jog, the dogs on either side of her.

Sophie reached the edge of the park and the busy thoroughfare lined with Hilo's downtown shops. She crossed that major artery and continued along it toward her apartment building, suddenly exhausted from all the emotion and the heavy meal. Her body was shutting down, telling her it needed a nap.

Things were so much different in her body now. The voice of the depression was a muted, distant whisper, while the little one inside clamored for its needs to be met.

She'd almost reached her apartment building, could even see its nearby cool cinderblock cube under the banyan tree, when a female voice called her name. "Sophie Ang."

Sophie turned her head.

Penny Chang stood beside a big green dumpster in an alley directly opposite her. The short, plump PR agent wore a fitted knee-length muumuu, rhinestone-studded sandals, a hibiscus in her sleek updo—and had a silenced pistol pointed at Sophie.

Penny still reminded Sophie of a sweet female Buddha. The gun seemed cartoonlike, a "one of these things does not belong" element from a child's illustration in a magazine Sophie had seen in a doctor's office.

"What do you want?" Sophie let go of the dogs' leashes, hoping the two would realize something was amiss—but they saw no threat in the woman Sophie was speaking to. The Lab and the pit bull galloped away with home in sight.

"I want a little payback for the way you screwed me and my cousin over." Penny gestured with the pistol. "Come closer. Into the alley."

"So you can shoot me out of sight?" Sophie was too far from the woman to mount any kind of attack, and she hadn't brought her own weapon. She'd thought she was safe.

But she was never safe. Bitterness tightened her throat.

"I can shoot you from here, just fine," Penny said. "But I'd like to talk to you, first."

Sophie's gaze flicked to the side. The dogs had reached the apartment building and were running up the exterior stairs. They were headed for Jake's place! Maybe he was there, maybe they could get his attention…

She had to buy time. "Tell me why you're doing this."

"Because I'm being investigated for embezzling funds from the Merrie Monarch Festival. You and your partner pretended to be customers and fingered me! Did you think I didn't recognize you from the news as the witness against Akane? And now, you shot my cousin." Penny took a step closer. The black bore of her pistol seemed to expand in Sophie's visual field.

"Killing me doesn't accomplish anything."

"It accomplishes me feeling better about all the shit that's gone down." Penny took another step toward Sophie. The woman's hand was steady, her gaze unwavering. She was going to shoot Sophie; she just wanted a little privacy to do it.

Sophie raised her hands so that anyone watching could see that she was in trouble. "I refuse to make it easy for you." She took a step backward.

"Oh yeah, you will, or I'll shoot you in the gut and you can die slowly, right here."

The baby would die first.

If only she could slow things down. Every moment of life was a moment of opportunity, a moment for things to change. She'd learned that out on the lava when she wrestled with death and came out the victor.

"I'm not going anywhere. I guess I'll die right here in public, then." Sophie dropped to her knees and put her hands on her head. Her eyes felt hot and her gaze filled with power as she cursed Penny with the only weapon she had: her words. "I'm pregnant. May my child haunt you forever. May your dreams be filled with screams and your womb be cursed, barren, and a source of death. *Foul daughter of the devil!*"

A flicker of something showed in Penny's face for the first time —disgust? Regret? Fear? The woman had obviously never killed before. She was having to work up to it, and her mouth flattened into a line of determination. "I don't give a shit what you say."

Penny was close enough now that Sophie could see the woman's finger tightening on the trigger.

Sophie shut her eyes—and a blow from the side slammed her to the ground, knocking the wind out of her.

The thunder of gunfire overhead caused Sophie to draw in her knees and curl her arms over her head, trying to shield herself—but another body was already on top of her, protecting her.

The barrage stopped.

Even through the odor of gunshot residue, Sophie recognized Jake's unique scent and the heft and feel of his body on hers—but the heavy form on top of her didn't move.

"Jake!" Sophie screamed his name but couldn't hear it through the ringing of her ears, deafened by the gunshots. She wriggled out from under his body, scanning to see if Penny was still a threat—but the woman was crumpled on the ground, her pistol still in her hand. Sophie ran over and kicked the weapon away, then returned to crouch over Jake's still form.

Blood poured down his face, obscuring it. His arm was extended, his weapon fallen from an unresponsive hand.

"Jake! Jake, no!" Sophie dropped to the ground and drew his head into her lap, heedless of the blood, and wept.

CHAPTER FORTY-TWO

Hot copper smell.

Pounding in his head, like waves. Surf swishing through his brain, erasing thought, memory, self.

Sobbing.

Loud, wretched sobbing, like someone had run over a puppy. *Something bad had happened.*

Sorrow suffused him.

Jake wished he could make the crying stop. Life hurt a lot, and no one told you that when you were a kid.

His head was pillowed on something soft—*a lap.*

A firm thigh under his cheek, arms around his shoulders. There were even breasts nearby, brushing him occasionally.

"Heaven." He rubbed his face back and forth in the softness touching him. He dragged the logy weights of his arms up to encircle the thighs, buttocks and waist of the angel greeting him on the other side.

The crying stopped.

"Jake?" His angel was Sophie. She was wiping at his face with her shirt, crying again but in a happy way, and kissing him, little pecks that felt like raindrops. "I thought you were dead. I thought she shot you."

"Not heaven?" Vague disappointment. However, waking up with his face nuzzled into the crotch of the woman he loved suited Jake's idea of paradise just fine.

"Not yet. Not for a long time." Sophie's voice shook with fervor.

The sound of sirens. Voices. Hands. Moving. Jake groaned. His eyes were shut with something sticky—blood. He couldn't get them open, couldn't see.

"You're gonna be fine, Mr. Dunn. Bullet grazed your skull. Head wounds bleed a lot. Just relax."

"Sophie?" *He needed his angel.* She had to stay with him. "Sophie!"

"I'm here, Jake. I'll ride with you." She squeezed his fingers, hard.

Memories flashed as they lifted him onto something soft and rolled him forward.

He'd been agonizing over Sophie's text, deciding what it meant, what he would do, how to talk to her. The dogs, suddenly scratching and yelping outside his apartment.

Opening the door. Something was wrong—where was Sophie?

Looking straight across the street at Sophie. She was talking to someone in the alley that he couldn't see. She raised her hands slowly. *Someone had her at gunpoint.*

Jake didn't have to fetch his weapon because it was always on him. He must have run and jumped down three flights of stairs and crossed the road, but he didn't remember that.

The next memory was Sophie, ahead of him on the sidewalk. She'd dropped to her knees. Her hands were on her head, and she was cursing in Thai.

He flew through the air, slamming into her body, flattening her beneath him, already firing into the alley.

Firing blind at whoever was there.

More lifting. The rattle of wheels, the clang of metal, voices overhead. But Sophie was still holding his hand. That was important.

Something else was important. Something… "The baby?"

"The baby's fine. I'm fine. You saved us."

"Good." Jake relaxed. Darkness swallowed him up.

CHAPTER FORTY-THREE

Sᴏᴘʜɪᴇ ᴡᴏᴋᴇ to the rustle and squeak of the nurse's shoes on the floor as she moved around Jake, checking his vitals. The hospital room was dim and cool, lit solely by LED lighting on the floor and the various beeping monitors.

Jake was still in a medically induced coma. "Your boyfriend has a hard head," the brain surgeon on duty had told her after assessing Jake's injury. "But even hard heads can get too much pressure inside, and that bullet creased him good. We'll keep him knocked out a while until the swelling has a chance to go down. He's a very lucky man."

And Sophie was a very lucky woman. There was no doubt he'd saved her and her baby's life, without a thought to his own safety.

Sophie had fallen asleep on the chair in the corner of the room, a chair with a handy pullout for her feet. Someone had covered her with a blue polyester blanket during the night, and she was grateful for its warmth, tugging the covering tight around her as she scooted the chair closer to Jake. She leaned against his bed and rested her cheek on his hand, longing for him to be awake, to touch her with that hand.

She was thankful for the quiet, for the privacy restriction of the unit Jake was in. She'd been stuck in the waiting room for hours while Jake was assessed and stabilized.

Felicia had brought in a bag containing a change of clothing and toiletries for each of them. "I hope he's okay," Felicia had said, handing over the duffel. "I'll take care of the dogs for you, and I've already called Mr. Hamilton and Mr. Bix and let them know what happened."

Sophie had been so focused on Jake she hadn't paid attention to the EMTs working on the woman who'd created the situation in the first place. "Penny Chang?"

Felicia shook her head. "She didn't make it."

Sophie felt nothing but relief. "Thanks, Felicia. You're the best."

"I just…hope Jake is all right." The young woman raised shining eyes to Sophie. Her feelings were obvious. "He's such a great guy."

"Yes, he is. And I intend to make sure he knows it," Sophie said. "I'll call you if we need anything else. Mahalo for holding down the fort, as they say."

"You're welcome." Felicia shifted from foot to foot. "So, you and Jake…"

"We're together, Felicia." *God, she hoped they were.* Sophie held the girl's eyes with a compassionate gaze. "I hope that won't be a problem at the office."

Felicia straightened. "Nope. I get it." She spun on a heel, and if she was crying as she hurried away down the hall, she had too much pride to let it show.

Sophie picked up Jake's hand in the darkened room. *Unusual for it to be so relaxed, open.* Jake was always in motion, those hands at work, at play, in use all the time. And it had been way too long since they'd touched her, held her, loved her—and she, him.

Sophie traced the calluses at the base of Jake's fingers, the thickened skin in the web of his thumb. *All of the places a weapon touched.*

Each of the men she'd loved, and she could admit now that there had been three, had such different calluses—but *this* was the hand she chose, she wanted, she needed. She kissed the hardened skin. Her eyes closed, breathing him in.

"My angel is still here." Jake's voice above Sophie was a hoarse croak.

"Jake!" Sophie stood swiftly, checking the monitors.

All of the beeping seemed normal. The doctor had told her he'd wake naturally when the swelling in his skull had gone down enough. She brought her gaze to Jake's shadowed face, leaning over to kiss him gently. His lips felt like marble. She wanted to kiss them longer and warm them up. "I would have been an angel for sure if you hadn't done what you did. How are you feeling?"

"Like I got shot in the head." He groaned, raising the hand that wasn't clutching hers to touch the thick bandage covering one side of his skull. "Feels like someone's playing the bongos in there."

Sophie began to sit back down, but he sidled over in the bed and opened his arm. "Can you come up here?"

"Of course." Sophie's pulse pounded with hope—he wanted her close! She climbed onto the bed, awkward with all of his monitors, tucking herself alongside him in a tight fit. They both emitted a sigh of contentment as she settled in. Sophie's eyes drifted shut as Jake's heat penetrated, melting her like wax into boneless contentment. *He was always so warm.*

Long moments went by as their breathing fell into sync.

"I have something to say." Jake's voice was more of a rumbling vibration than anything else, but Sophie tensed.

"We can talk later. When you're feeling better." The news about Alika being the baby's father felt like a weight on her chest.

"No. I have to say this now." Jake shifted her, groaned as his head was jostled, but persisted, positioning Sophie so that he could look into her face. "I've had time to think. About everything."

Sophie stiffened further. "Please. Let's do this when you're better. You should rest."

Jake's eyes were caves of shadow; she wished she could see the expression in them. "I've had time to take a long, hard look at myself and my issues. And what I've decided is this: I don't care who the baby's father is. I love you. And I love the baby because it's part of you." Jake's free hand slid around to cup her breast. "These are bigger, you know. I spotted that right away."

Relief swamped Sophie, but she was about to put his words to the test. She wriggled as his thumb found her sensitive nipple. "I have to tell you the news about the baby's father."

"I guessed that was why you texted me. And I guessed it's Alika's baby, because you didn't just tell me right off the bat." He sounded matter-of-fact.

"And still you took a bullet for me. For *us*." Sophie pushed the button on the bed that turned on the light. *She had to see his face.*

"And I'd do it again in a heartbeat." Jake's eyes were sunk in puffy lids, their silver color muted by the swelling distorting his face —but his gaze was unwavering, warm and loving on hers.

"I wish the baby were yours," she whispered.

"It would have been nice." Jake leaned forward to kiss her. "But it truly doesn't matter." His hand was still wandering, and now it rested gently on the grapefruit-sized hardness just beginning to reshape her abdomen. "This kid is going to have the best of both worlds—Alika's awesome home and family, and you and me, too."

Tears slid down Sophie's cheeks. "I love you. I should have told you a long time ago, but I was uncertain. Afraid. I've made so many mistakes."

"You know, my sister told me how to deal with a woman like you." Jake snuggled Sophie closer, stroking her body from breast to hip, heating her up in spite of the hospital bed's impedimenta. "She said not to be needy. To be so good you'd want to be with me."

"Your sister is a wise woman," Sophie said, and kissed him.

CHAPTER FORTY-FOUR

THE EDITH KANAKAʻOLE Stadium seemed to vibrate from within like a giant drum, as the male dancers spun in perfect unison. The slap and thump of bare feet was emphasized by the percussion of *ipu* and chant, resonating in a silence held by the crowd, a bowl containing the performance. Skin gleamed over muscle and bone, and crisp, powerful movement gave an almost martial arts feel to the *kane* hula, the men's stabbing motions of arms and hands warlike and riveting.

Connor sat beside Sophie in the front row, his eyes recording the amazing sight of the Merrie Monarch competition in full swing, but his real attention was on the woman beside him.

Sophie was holding Jake's hand as he sat next to her. Both of their faces were turned up toward the stage, their eyes glued to the dancers, expressions rapt.

The two were together again. Reconciled. The whole drama was resolving beautifully—except for him.

Connor's eyes lingered on the couple's joined hands, resting in Sophie's lap close against her waist—so that both of them were touching the tiny one nestled there.

Jake was okay. The child was healthy so far. Sophie was happy.

A deep contentment filled Connor. He was a hawk soaring above, watching for danger and opportunity. Guarding his people. Making things right. He was important and needed. If he was on the outside, he had no one to blame but himself. He accepted that, now.

The performance reached a crescendo as the dancers leaped and landed, in perfect accord, with a thump that rocked the stage.

Wild cheering, louder than a football game, filled the room as the dancers bowed.

Connor twitched in surprise as Sophie touched his hand with her free one. He flicked her a glance: cheeks pink, tears shimmering in her eyes. "Isn't it incredible?" The sound and energy of the room were so intense that he was reading her lips.

He smiled, gazing at her. "Incredible."

Turn the page for a sneak peek of, *Wired Courage*, Paradise Crime Thrillers book 9.

SNEAK PEEK
WIRED COURAGE, PARADISE CRIME THRILLERS BOOK 9

Discipline was beautiful, even when it hurt.

Pim Wat stood on the stone balcony of the temple overlooking the courtyard. Rows of acolytes, dressed identically in black cotton *gi,* practiced before their master. The crisp movements of the closely guarded martial arts routine were already embedded in her own muscle memory, and if she'd joined the young men and women in their tidy rows, she could have performed their routine perfectly, too.

Someone missed a movement, the mistake glaring in the crisp rows of conformity, and the master raised his baton.

All movement ceased. The rows of recruits froze into stillness. The master lowered the baton, and the recruits dropped to the ground to do push-ups.

They would do push-ups until he raised the baton again.

Armita appeared at Pim Wat's elbow. "Your tea, mistress."

Pim Wat took the hand thrown porcelain teacup without looking at her maid. She sniffed the jasmine-scented brew, then took a sip. Scalding hot, just as she preferred. "Acceptable."

She seated herself on one of two chunks of amethyst that had been beveled into stools. A large tiger's-eye plinth, glowing with bronze iridescence, served as a table. Armita faded back into the building after leaving a lacquered tray holding a pot and another teacup.

Perhaps the master would join her, but he didn't always. Pim Wat willed him to, craving the drug of his presence.

The recruits were still doing push-ups. At last, the master raised his baton, and they leapt to their feet in one accord. He barked out an order, and the routine began again. He tapped a student on the end of one of the rows with the baton, handing it over. The black-clad young man took the carved ivory cane reverently, and stepped into the leader's place in front.

The master strode toward Pim Wat, and she smiled with satisfaction as he glanced up at her.

Moments later he seated himself on the other chunk of amethyst and picked up his teacup. He closed his eyes to savor the tea, some of the most expensive and exquisite in the world, as Pim Wat feasted her hungry gaze on the man that she loved with an unseemly and obsessive passion.

The master looked no more than thirty, though he was at least Pim Wat's age. His long black hair was braided and decorated with carved jade. The smooth fans of his eyelashes rested against golden-skinned, high cheekbones, contrasting with straight black brows. He opened dark purple eyes that must be the result of some multi-racial encounter of ancestors. "When is she coming to us?"

Pim Wat tightened her mouth in annoyance and hid her expression behind the delicate, hand thrown cup. "My daughter is stubborn. I've told you this."

"The Yām Khûmkạn requires her."

"And I've told you that she cannot be persuaded. Especially now that she's pregnant." Pim Wat's cup rattled as she set it on the tray. *She was going to be a grandmother*. What a reminder that time was passing. Despite all her efforts, she was getting old. "I have tried everything to get her to come, even threatening her lover. She has refused."

"Does she suspect anything about what we really want?"

"No. How could she? But she does not trust me." Pim Wat made a fist. "I cannot command her like I used to."

"You must manage your emotions, Beautiful One," the master said. He leaned toward her, but instead of a kiss, drew a line down her profile with a finger and tipped up her chin. He teased her, rolling the ball of his thumb across her lower lip. Pim Wat's eyes fluttered shut in anticipation and her body trembled. "Take her, if there is no other way. Do what you must do."

His touch disappeared.

Pim Wat kept her eyes closed for a long moment, still hoping, but when she opened them, he was gone.

"Manage my emotions, by Quan Yin's left tit," she snarled. "Armita! My tea is cold!"

Armita came out onto the balcony and whisked away the tea. Pim Wat looked down at the practice area, but it no longer entertained her. She followed her maid into the main chamber of her apartment.

Thick, luxurious carpets and rich silk drapes softened the harsh stone walls and floors of the ancient room. "We must prepare a plan to get Sophie Malee," Pim Wat said.

Armita's eyes flashed, just a tiny flare of defiance. "Are you sure that's a good idea, mistress? She is well protected."

"The master wants her, and thus she will come. Once she's here, they won't be able to take her back. The stronghold of the Yām Khûmkạn is too remote and fortified." Pim Wat turned toward a tall, exotic wood armoire. "Back to Hawaii I must go. Such a long, tiresome flight." Pim Wat pinched the back of Armita's arm viciously as the maid reached out to open the armoire. "And that's for questioning me."

Continue reading *Wired Courage*: tobyneal.net/WCweb

ACKNOWLEDGMENTS

Aloha dear readers!

One of my favorite moments in completing a book is when I get to write this letter to you. Thanks for being on this journey with Sophie and me!

I continue my exploration of *villains* in this book. Yes, Akane Chang may be a sadist, but he still has *feelings*. He grieves for his murdered family and swears revenge, as anyone might. Terence Chang (who first appears in *Twisted Vine* and *Fire Beach* of the Lei Crime Series) evolves, hosting a bloodbath to take leadership of the Chang empire. *Can you do evil in striving to do a greater good?* Terence is exploring that—and where will it end? Will he be able to do good out of his evil, or will his actions corrupt him further? Stay tuned!

Connor, as the Ghost, dances with that dilemma, too. It's a question that fascinates me.

And Pim Wat? Who knows with that woman! But one thing is sure—we haven't seen the last of Sophie's enigmatic mother or her intriguing sidekick, Armita.

I've long been fascinated and moved by the pageant, spectacle, and powerful cultural celebration that is the Merrie Monarch Festival, taking place every spring in Hilo, Hawaii. I've been talking about incorporating it into one of my stories for years, though I've never personally attended. It's a bucket list item!

Challenges with handling the subject matter, however, have kept me from doing so until now—the main one being that the Festival is something of a sacred cultural activity. I'd be loath to offend, however inadvertently, by misrepresenting any aspect. It's a tricky thing to be a *haole* and write about Hawaiian culture. I'm privileged to educate the public a bit through an entertaining story, but I do so with the utmost care, respect and even *awe*.

Awe is the feeling I get most when watching the Merrie Monarch Festival. (If you haven't seen it, search for it on YouTube or other video channels. You won't be sorry you did!) Because of that awe, though I knew the Merrie Monarch would be a fabulous centerpiece to build a mystery around, I didn't want to kill any dancers, desecrate any *heiaus*, or corrupt any *kumus*.

Because of those concerns, I went with a case of embezzlement by one of the evil Changs, a "safe" way to delve into the topic. I wasn't able to get into the intricacies of the Festival, competition procedure, judging, and hula practices due to that. Maybe someday, and another book... But even the few paragraphs I wrote describing the hula feel infused with *mana,* and I hope you feel that too.

Wow, this book! I was consumed with it! I couldn't plot using my usual outline. I felt my way through, chapter-by-chapter, unsure where I was going but allowing it to draw me relentlessly forward. I'm already writing the next one, *Wired Courage #9,* in the same way.

Sophie pregnant? What the heck?

Yes, there was a hint that appeared organically in *Wired Secret #7* that my brain, cued by the questions of readers, hatched into a huge plot element in this story. As I went with it, I realized that Sophie's pregnancy is the perfect vehicle for her healing. And Alika's. And Jake's, and Connor's, too. Babies often bring healing.

And just as often, terrible heartache.

All the way up to writing the scene where Sophie finds out who the baby's father is, I didn't know who it was going to be. Didn't know how I was going to tie up the relationships. And finally, the characters themselves told me, resolving themselves into an unconventional but functional "family," like so many blended ones in this modern age.

Thanks go out to my faithful copyeditors Don and Bonnie, and my typo hunters Angie and Shirley, and of course, to my indispensable business manager, Jamie Davis. You all keep me functioning and the books on track. Thanks also to Ihilani for your consult about the Festival, and Walt for helping with tech consult. It clearly takes a village!

If you enjoyed *Wired Fear #8*, would you take a few moments to write a review? They are so incredibly important to a book's success, and even a few words can make a big difference. Mahalo in advance for your support and sharing of the books!

I hope you'll continue Sophie's journey with me in *Wired Courage #9*. Excerpt follows.

Until next time, I'll be writing!

Much aloha,

FREE BOOKS

Join my mystery and romance lists and receive free, full-length, award-winning ebooks of *Torch Ginger & Somewhere on St. Thomas* as welcome gifts: tobyneal.net/TNNews

TOBY'S BOOKSHELF

PARADISE CRIME SERIES

Paradise Crime Mysteries
Blood Orchids
Torch Ginger
Black Jasmine
Broken Ferns
Twisted Vine
Shattered Palms
Dark Lava
Fire Beach
Rip Tides
Bone Hook
Red Rain
Bitter Feast
Razor Rocks
Wrong Turn
Shark Cove
Coming 2021

Paradise Crime Mysteries Novella
Clipped Wings

Paradise Crime Mystery
Special Agent Marcella Scott
Stolen in Paradise

Paradise Crime Suspense Mysteries
Unsound

Paradise Crime Thrillers
Wired In
Wired Rogue
Wired Hard
Wired Dark
Wired Dawn
Wired Justice
Wired Secret
Wired Fear
Wired Courage
Wired Truth
Wired Ghost
Wired Strong
Wired Revenge
Coming 2021

ROMANCES
Toby Jane

The Somewhere Series
Somewhere on St. Thomas
Somewhere in the City
Somewhere in California

The Somewhere Series
Secret Billionaire Romance
Somewhere in Wine Country
Somewhere in Montana
Date TBA
Somewhere in San Francisco
Date TBA

A Second Chance Hawaii Romance
Somewhere on Maui

Co-Authored Romance Thrillers
The Scorch Series
Scorch Road
Cinder Road
Smoke Road
Burnt Road
Flame Road
Smolder Road

YOUNG ADULT

Standalone
Island Fire

NONFICTION
TW Neal

Memoir
Freckled
Open Road

ABOUT THE AUTHOR

Kirkus Reviews calls Neal's writing, *"persistently riveting. Masterly."*

Award-winning, USA Today bestselling social worker turned author Toby Neal grew up on the island of Kaua`i in Hawaii. Neal is a mental health therapist, a career that has informed the depth and complexity of the characters in her stories. Neal's mysteries and thrillers explore the crimes and issues of Hawaii from the bottom of the ocean to the top of volcanoes. Fans call her stories, *"Immersive, addicting, and the next best thing to being there."*

Neal also pens romance, romantic thrillers, and writes memoir/non-fiction under TW Neal.

Visit tobyneal.net for more ways to stay in touch!
or
Join my Facebook readers group, *Friends Who Like Toby Neal Books,* for special giveaways and perks.

Made in the USA
Las Vegas, NV
19 January 2023

65868723R00152